This book is on loan from the
Mid York Library System

**When you are finished reading,
please return the book so
that others may enjoy it.**

The Mid York Library System is pleased
to partner with **CABVI** in assisting
those with special vision needs.

If you found the size of print in this book
helpful, there may be other ways
CABVI can help. Please call today toll
free at **1-877-719-9996**
or **(315) 797-2233.**

Central Association for the Blind and Visually Impaired

Mid York
LIBRARY SYSTEM

The Mistress

Philippe Tapon

The Mistress

WHEELER
PUBLISHING, INC.
ROCKLAND, MA

★ AN AMERICAN COMPANY ★

Published in Large Print by arrangement with Dutton, a member of
Penguin Putnam, Inc.

in the United States and Canada.

Wheeler Large Print Book Series.

Set in 16 pt Plantin.

Library of Congress Cataloging-in-Publication Data

Tapon, Philippe.
    The mistress / Philippe Tapon.
        p. (large print) cm.(Wheeler large print book series)
    ISBN 1-56895-725-4 (hardcover)
    1. France—History—German occupation, 1940-1945—Fiction. 2. World
War, 1939-1945—France—Paris—Fiction. 3. Mistresses—France—Paris—
Fiction. 4. Family—France—Fiction. 5. Avarice—Fiction. 6. Historical
fiction. gsafd. 7. Large type books. I. Title. II. Series
[PS3570.A5678M57   1999]
813'.54—dc21
                                                          99-022154
                                                              CIP

to Billy

PART ONE

Paris, 1944

CHAPTER ONE

My grandfather had a mistress named Simone. She lived with him in the flat adjoining his medical offices, on the rue de Maubeuge; she was his secretary, and wore black skirts that made her legs seem white and fresh.

The Nazis had taken over the city, food was rationed, but Emile Bastien, and his son, and daughter, and his mistress, ate well: eggs, good beef, good bread at a time when everything was stale and hard and hard to find. Emile had devised a treatment for stomach disorders involving something like shock therapy. Patients who had gotten sick on war food would lie down in his cabinet, and he, with long white delicate fingers, would run over their bellies, asking them, Does it hurt here? The patients trusted the soft hands, and by the time they had been conditioned to the soft jokes Emile was making ("How can they win the war if they can't make an éclair au chocolat?") they had not noticed the instruments—the dials, the voltmeters behind them—crackle and glow with an electrical red. Doctor Bastien would apply a light goo, a pink fluid not unlike a woman's fluids—and then he would affix to the skin a disc, shining with all the lights of the office, connected as if by a metallic umbilical cord to a mother-box of electrical batteries.

"Think of something pleasant now," the doctor said.

"Pleasant?"

"Yes, pleasant. The south, for instance."

"Well, you know, I'm from Aix, and the shittiest thing these pigs have done is stop us from going down there. Fuckers! You'd think that even in a goddamn *occupied* country we could visit our fucking families, eh, *docteur?*"

"Think of something *pleasant* now."

"Mighty few pleasant things to think of now. Pleasant? When I was a kid... I used to live on a farm in Aix..."

"Yes—go on," said Emile, ready to crank the current, his hand on the menacing round, smooth knob.

"Oh, Aix. There were horses. And hay. Oh! the smell of the hay. Do you know it, Doctor, the countryside? Hey! What are you doing?"

"Relax, please. Tell me about the hay. I don't know the countryside so well. Although my wife, she does.... She lives in Perpignan, you see."

"It feels awfully sinister, what you're doing down there. Still, my girl—you remember her—pretty girl! wonderful girl!—she said it felt funny, your treatment. Are you really shocking my poor stomach?"

"Not shocking. A term for vulgarians. In fact what I am actually doing is applying a *very* low voltage in order to stimulate gastric cells. My theory—you may read about it, if you care to, in *Le Journal de Médecine*—is that gastric cells, like heart cells or other *muscular* cells, can be stimulated after arrest by the miracle of electricity. Of course, they can also be silenced, shut down, tranquilized—

4

fascinating variations on a theme. Like Mozart. Do you like Mozart?"

"No. Where are you from, Doctor?"

"The west."

"And you came to Paris—"

"Only a few years ago. I did my schooling in—"

"Hey, that hurts!"

"Now. Ahem! Yes, *now* is the moment of great tension. Nevertheless, the tension must rise. Higher and higher. Until tissue enervation takes place. You must endeavor to keep calm. At all costs, you must not move, or shift the electrodes. You will damage your stomach or possibly electrocute yourself. Pray, talk to me about something which relaxes you."

"Oh! God!"

"Talk, talk, man—about—your girl, say."

"Oh! God! Easy for you to say! Fellow's frying my stomach and I've got to tell him all about my girl! What do you want to know? You've seen her!"

"Please—keep talking." The patient was wincing, eyes shut tight, fighting back tears. "Sing a song, if you like."

" 'Ah—vous—di—rai—' " he sang, between gasps. "I can't!" he yelled.

"Oh, tut-tut-tut. I'll tell your girlfriend what a sissy you are. She held up under *much* higher voltage. She did not cry or even show pain. Not even in the slightest. Brave girl."

The man's face became stern as stone. He sang, loudly, clearly: " 'Frère Jacques, frère Jacques...' "

"Yes, yes! Good, good! Keep singing!"

" 'Dormez-vous? Dormez-vous? Sonnez les matines! Sonnez les matines! Ding! dang! dong! Ding! dang! dong!' " The man winced again in suppressed agony.

"Five!" Emile began counting melodramatically, holding a hand up like a starting gun. "Four! Three! Two and a half! Two! One! There! Off! Isn't that better?"

"Oh-la-la! Oh-la-la!" The man fairly collapsed. "Thought I was going to die there."

"My dear, poor fellow. You'd better not say more, or people will hear stories about how you were whimpering in here like a little dog."

"Oh, go on."

Doctor Bastien went over to his great desk and made some brisk jottings with a fountain pen. Scratch, scratch, scratch went the pen, while horses and autos clippity-clopped and vroomed outside in the street.

"Did you say your wife was in Perpignan?" asked the man, still bare chested. He tugged gently at the nipples of steel affixed to his chest, as if to encourage the doctor to take them off.

"Yes, she is," replied the doctor, without looking up or interrupting his notes in the slightest.

"Have you been down? I mean—since the beginning of the Occupation?"

"Just once."

"How was it?"

Doctor Bastien stopped, looked into space, thinking of the right word. "*Rewarding,*" he finally said.

"Is it like the old France?" asked the man.

"Yes," replied the doctor. "It's the same old stupid France. Killing Krauts one minute, half in love with Hitler the next."

"I'm not."

Emile looked up. "No," he said. "I see." Emile put down his pen, drummed his fingers on the tabletop, and steepled his fingers. "Hmmm... it'd be fascinating, you know, to see the gastric disturbances suffered by the collabos, and the disturbances suffered by the Resistance. I'd bet you they'd be completely different. Hmm. It'd be an interesting study to do, when the war is over of course. Assuming there are any Resistants left. Hmph! Maybe the Nazis should save a few, just for such medical, psychiatric purposes. Would you say a Resistant has a strong stomach? Or no stomach for the Nazis? Tragic. The Reich is doing such a good job eliminating Jews, perhaps they'll take on stomach disorders next. Put me out of business," he added with a half-smile.

The man stared down at his belly, still coupled to the infernal machine. "Can I take these off?"

"I'll take them off for you," said Emile, suiting the action to the word. They slid off gently, like hose from a leg, and Emile plunged them into a stainless-steel sink. "For disinfection," he added. "Do you know this is the first stainless-steel sink in Paris? From America. If only the imbeciles here listened to Pasteur, they'd give up their bloody precious porcelain." From a counter he took a spotless rag and wiped his fingers immaculately. Not a thread of his dark suit was soiled. "Mademoiselle Givry!" he called.

His secretary—his mistress—entered. She wore a dark, austere outfit, and yet moved from side to side like a snake; her lips were arranged like the petals of a rose. There was witchcraft in her walk.

"Oui, docteur?"

"Monsieur Andrieux is almost ready." She looked at the man, bare chested on the table. Their gaze was electric for a moment, and then she pulled back.

"Your wife?" the patient asked after she had gone.

"No—my secretary."

"Ah."

"Your payment."

"It's—outside, in the bag. The big gray bag."

"You'll excuse me for a moment."

In the cabinet the patient thought, What a damn good-looking woman! And then Emile came back.

"This bag?"

"Yes."

Emile opened it and looked. "Thank you. This cheese is hard to find."

"Only the best for you, Doctor. My girl told me you were a miracle worker."

"Piffle. If within three days you are still experiencing difficulty digesting, I shall see you again."

"Free, of course."

"No, because your ailment may be of a different nature than I diagnosed, and there is no way to tell besides applying treatment."

"Times are tough, Doctor."

"I have to eat as well as you do."

"I won't come back if I have to pay."

"If you don't come back when you don't get better, you won't be able to eat, I assure you. Sir. Good day."

The man stood up and mumbled, "*Au revoir.*"

As the patient walked down the steps, both doctor and secretary would have sworn he was whistling "La Marseillaise," but then the tune dissolved and became something else.

Weekends, the doctor, his son, his daughter, and his mistress would go to a semi-country house in the suburbs, in La Varenne. The house and its plot covered several hectares. Going in and out of the city in Grandfather's immense Chenard-Walker sixty-horsepower engine—quite a vroom in those days—the four would have to present Occupation papers to the Nazis at the city gates: and they were out of the city for a weekend rest. Grandfather always drove: Simone put on a hat, sometimes with white flowers on the brim, almost drooping like a bridal veil into her eyes, and René and Paulette bickered in the back.

"Mine!"

"No!"

"Maman!" René wailed.

Grandfather would watch the road unfurl, imperturbable. Simone wore a nearly-smiling mouth almost like a brooch. Emile had always imagined that kept women wore hard faces, imperious chins, had demanding cheekbones; but Simone's face was like a toughening adolescent's: like a very brave girl about to dive into a cold pool, hoping by sheer hard joy to keep the cold from her heart.

"So—we're going to swim, eh, kids?" Grandfather said.

"Eh?" René said, almost neighing with incredulity.

"René, speak with more respect to your father," said Simone.

Grandfather's gaze had become as hard and long as the road.

"Eh?" René said again.

"Don't say 'Eh!' " said Paulette.

"Eeeeeeeeeeeeeee!"

"That's enough!" said the doctor. Silence. "Sometimes, I do not know what to do with this... clown."

"Emile, he's a child. It's normal."

"I was not this way."

"He is different from you. Right, René?"

"Eeeeeeeeeeeeee!"

"Enough!" bellowed Grandfather. He pulled the Chenard-Walker over to the side of the road. His face was dark as thunderclouds, and he raised a large white pale hand in front of his face.

"*Une fois de plus et je te gifle. Tu as compris?*" One more time and... you understand?

10

René nodded his little head three little times to indicate that yes, he understood. Grandfather shot a gaze full of Jesuitical persecution, full of imaginary blows and fire, and then turned forward and re-entered the road.

René crossed his arms and sulked to show he wasn't going to say anything, and that he hated not being able to say anything. Paulette, beside him, leaned back in her seat, put her hand beneath her chin, let the wind play with the front of her hair, and smiled sardonically into the wind. She waited until her brother saw her in this attitude. It was an imitation of Simone's attitude in front.

"You see?" said Emile, to the boy. "Why can't you be like your sister?"

Because I'm a boy, thought René, but he pointedly said nothing.

"She is always so quiet and thoughtful, eh? Why can't you be more like that?"

Paulette went on being the damnable princess, continuing with her Simone imitation. She brushed her hair with her hands, opening and closing her mouth, primping, primping.

"Quit it!" hissed René to his sister.

"C'est bien, ma fille." That's good, my daughter, said the doctor.

In the dining room at La Varenne, an inscription ran round the room. *"Toi, quiconque soit, bienvenu. Prends place à table, boit, et raconte-nous les choses merveilleuses."* Meaning, "You, whosoever you are, welcome. Take your place

11

at table, drink, and tell us wonderful things."

There were two thronelike chairs in which Paulette and René, in their children's games, would play king and queen. The crown of each chair had a carving that looked like two sperm chasing each other; on each handrest a lion crouched, head blazing, teeth drawn back. A child could run his fingers through the wooden jaw, through the harmless fangs. Buttons like metal flowers ran round the sides and back of the throne, holding the velours in place; when you ran your hand over the fabric one way, it felt bristly, rough, and fought back; the other way, it was smooth and surrendered. The eyes of the lions had no pupils; it was easy to pretend they were buttons activating long, far-off things. The chairs were each in corners, dark and mysterious, and were good hiding places from adults. Children could see each other easily, though.

Cache-cache—hide-and-seek—was a game played almost every weekend, winter weekends especially, while the war wore on on the radio. Simone and Emile would listen to the radio.... Bulletins came in from Pétain, from Vichy, from Berlin, blared, and blared on, and on, but once—

Général de Gaulle entered the room through the wireless, staticky, haughty, and defiant. René was hiding in a closet. He was waiting for his sister to give up, and then to come out bursting at her, when he heard this voice fill the house, as if a stranger had entered.

"> > >"

He heard Paulette ask, "Who is it?" Emile turned down the volume. René knew then it was the wireless.

"Go to the window, Paulette. Make sure no one is outside. Keep watching," Emile commanded.

Oh, Paulette thought, this is far more fun than any childish game! This is real! "No one," she said, keeping watch by the window.

"> > >"

Precisely at this moment, René, feeling the moment could not be better, burst from his closet hiding place, screaming, "Here I am!"

Simone cried out; she thought it was the Gestapo. Even Emile yelled, and he flushed, slapped René across the face, and yelled, "What the *hell*! What's wrong with you?! Eh?!"

René started crying. Emile, furious, yelled, "Get out! Get *out* of here! This is *de Gaulle* we're trying to listen to!"

"Emile, shut up!" Simone screamed. "Someone will hear!"

René, crying, wailing like an ambulance siren, ran from the room, from the radio reading commands.

"Coast is clear," said Paulette, still at the window.

"What is *wrong* with your brother? Paulette?"

"My brother?" she answered incredulously. "He wants his mother."

Simone looked at Paulette defiantly. "Don't say that," she said.

"Listen!" ordered Emile.

"> > >."

13

● ● ●

Dinner that night, by wartime standards, was extraordinary. Because customers—patients—thought a stomach doctor would be particularly careful about what he ate, and because of the shortage of cash and coupons, they often paid him with choice, fatty cuts of beef, Chateaubriands, sometimes veal; or difficult-to-get cheeses, like Brie or Camembert or Roquefort. Plus, the house at La Varenne had a forty-hectare garden, and during the week, the single, aged, widowed servant—dressed in black, perhaps because it stirred less excitement from the SS—watered the potatoes, the vegetables, the lettuce, the fennel, the beans. The garden was never as productive as Emile thought it should be, and small wonder: his servant ripped up the best vegetables to sell on the black market.

"Paulette, go get your brother. The food is going to get cold."

"Are you *still* playing *cache-cache*?" asked Simone.

"No, we stopped playing *hours* ago," said Paulette. She went up to René's bedroom. "René?" She knocked. "It's dinnertime, so if you want to eat, Papa says to come down at once."

"I don't *want* to eat," said René.

"He doesn't want to eat," said his sister, back down at table.

"More for us," said Emile.

Emile said grace—so as to be heard upstairs: "FOR WHAT *WE* ARE ABOUT TO

14

RECEIVE, LET US BE *GRATEFUL*!" And they began eating, Emile deliberately helping himself to the meat which would have been his son's.

"What did you think of de Gaulle?" the father asked Paulette.

"Wait, let me close the shades," said Simone.

And on they talked, in excited whispers, about de Gaulle's crackling transmission. Upstairs, René's stomach was cursing his pride. He put his ear to the door; hearing nothing, he dared to steal into the carpeted corridor: he peered over the balustrade of the staircase, once, quickly, furtively, like a spy, then slid around like a snake to the first steps and as gently as water dribbling down started to move down the staircase. Suddenly, he was face to face with his father!

"Nothing for you. Hunger till tomorrow."

But René had already run up the stairs, gone to his room, locked himself in tight, as if he were running from the SS.

That was a long night of hunger. In his sheets he twisted; pushed in the cavity of his stomach, to see if hunger could be squeezed out; he thought of food, to see if that would help, but his belly growled at that torture; he tried not to think of that food, but he couldn't help it.

The house was quiet. He had heard his father and Simone kiss Paulette goodnight, and Paulette kiss them, and their respective doors clack shut. Very carefully, very slowly, after the light from the hall had stopped seeping in, he creaked open the door, peered outside, and on mouse feet pattered over the carpet to the bathroom. He ran the water a minute and then drank several bellyfuls of warm water. That would be food tonight. Then, as if returning to prison, he crept back like a gray shadow to his room, shut the door, thought of his mother.

Emile was staring at the lamp fixture in the ceilings, its circles of light, its plaster configurations, its molded decorative dance. He hardened his mouth, twitched his lips like an iron shuttle from side to side. A bolt came down in his soul. "What shall I do with him?"

"Maybe you could send him to boarding school."

"René? In a boarding school? No, I don't trust them." A long sigh of sadness came up from his chest, like a saw rending an old tree. The bed felt damp and hot. "Besides, all the French boarding schools would be controlled by the Nazis, and I'm not sure I want René there, much as he needs to be disciplined. Switzerland? Oh, it must be heaven! Real mountains instead of the imbecile Maginot Line. Switzerland! The entire rest of the continent is in love with war. What do Germans and French do, except quarrel? Like a marriage that isn't working? Oh, Simone, Simone, why, why did I ever marry?"

"Emile..."

"These children were a mistake. Better they had never been born. I was tricked, Simone, like a peasant! Oh, of all my mistakes *that* was the worst. Is that why it's sacred? Because it's always a mistake? Not like..."

Simone looked at him; her black hair framed her face; she took his hand. "We've come a long way since the Jesuits, yes?" She stroked his hand softly. "Wretched man, you've had a lot to suffer."

He said nothing. "My suffering is so little next to the good I know."

Simone looked up, then away, into the brown darkness of the bedroom. She heard the light pitter-patter of feet, ghostly feet, moving in darkness outside the door.

"I think it's a ghost," she said, thinking of someone else.

"Has it gone downstairs, this ghost?"

"No..." she said. She looked at Emile; his face was set like stone and his eyes were dry as dirt. Simone thought: she has gone south, this ghost. She is waiting alone. The ghost wonders what has happened to her children. The ghost haunts her house, her vineyards, her gardens, alone, with flat faces like more ghosts looking out from every corner of the phantom house: phantom, because she had never visited it.

"Do you think René understands?"

"Paulette understands."

"What do you think she thinks?"

"Well, she doesn't much like her mother anyway. I think she prefers you," he said, laughing quickly.

"And René?"

"René *must* understand."

"Is that a fact? Or a command?"

"How can he *not* understand? That would be the last straw, having to explain *you.*"

Simone fixed him with a cold stare. An Antarctic wind blew over the conversation.

"Marvelous how you never feel ready to *explain* me. Fabulous, how your feelings can never be justified. Whatever happens in your life has to be *rational.*"

"Simone... don't get started."

"Who's starting anything? I'm just your secretary. I start your coffee. I start all sorts of things. Not children, though. That I leave for *other* women."

Emile turned around crisply. "Simone..."

"Maybe the poor child wants his poor mother. Maybe he's unhappy here? Maybe he doesn't like me?"

"Oh, Simone, don't be ridiculous."

"Marvelous how he never speaks to me. Flattering how he ignores me, pretends I don't exist. I suppose all secretaries get treated so by their bosses' sons; yet there is a particular intensity in his noninterest which really is rather commendable. Maybe beneath the clownish demeanor there's a bourgeois snob waiting to come out."

Emile's face turned to granite.

"Are you listening, Emile?"

"Yes, Simone, I'm listening. Go on. It's fascinating."

She looked at him, and her lips quivered, quickened an instant. "You don't love me, do you, letting your awful son treat me as if I were some slut. Some pretty whore that you picked up off the street, some little wounded clever girl, some pretty piece of... snatch...."

She started crying.

"Oh, shush, shush, shush," Emile said. She went on crying. "Oh, God," Emile groaned, looking toward the crucifix that hung in his bedroom.

Simone went on crying, sobbing, gasping. "It's all I ask of you... all I ask of him. No one takes care of you like I do. How, where, do I *fail*?" She continued sobbing, her face hidden by a slanted hand, her fingers wrenched, curled. "Emile... the boy is impossible. Not just difficult—*impossible*! He's poisoning the house with his sick tricks, his boyish whisperings. He steals money and sends it to his mother!"

"Money?"

Simone was breathing more steadily now; her breath was shooting like weaponry finally deployed; there was satisfaction in having launched this accusation, as if the tight bowstrings of her resentments had snapped back to relaxation.

"Money. I can't prove it. But I suspect."

"*My* money! You're *sure*?"

Simone looked doubtful, intimidated, beneath this interrogation. "I can't—be sure."

"But—you *suspect*?"

She looked down.

"You have reason to believe—?"

She couldn't lie—but she nodded: the falsest yes.

CHAPTER TWO

The next morning, in the medical office, a priest in a cassock came to have his stomach treated. The cassock swished and swayed as he moved about the room, and the rectangle of light at his collar glowed like an amulet. His shoes shone.

"Good morning, Father Nicolas," said Emile, coming into the waiting room. The priest stood as if to attention. "You are too *early*! I'm supposed to have another patient now—but he hasn't arrived. You look well."

"Oh, pfui. Whited sepulchre. I'm dissolving inside."

"Painful?"

"Murder. An acid has dropped down into my tubes and is chewing inside me as we speak. I am doing penance—for gluttony, I suspect."

"Oh, pfui yourself—you're no glutton. Father?"

"I've *longings* for food. They cut our rations again. I think they are deliberately trying to starve—"

"Ah, wait—the bell—this is the other patient—maybe you'd like to wait with Simone, my sec—"

The door opened with a twist of a gloved hand. The other patient walked in.

It was a Schutzstaffel major: his uniform crisp and black, with the SS silver skull in place and an armband with a regimental name. Jacket, trousers, all fit as tightly as a glove, the all-swallowing black, the Nazi silver, gleaming and glaring in the brown light of the waiting room. The major looked down at the priest and the doctor's white jacket. The priest was sitting, angular and lean under the robes, while the doctor was standing with hands in the air, when this black angel darkened his door.

"Good morning." The major raised a hand.

"Good morning," said Emile, and saluted.

"Heil," said the priest, twisting the diphthong to make it sound like the American "*hi.*" And he remained sitting.

"It appears I am a bit late." His French was perfect. "Shall I wait? Have you smuggled a patient in before me?"

"Nein, mein Herr," Emile answered, in German. "We can see you now."

"Good." Then, to the priest: "I am sorry indeed if your suffering is *so* great you cannot *stand* when you salute."

"Well, God bless you, my child."

The major's stare went from cold to icy, and when he finally disengaged a stalactite snapped in the silence.

"This way," said the doctor.

The major passed the desk where Simone worked. "Bonjour, mademoiselle," he said, smiling.

She smiled back. "Bonjour, mein Herr."

"Please sit down," said Emile to the major, having arrived in the operating chamber. The major, still wearing his hat, gleaming, glinting in the light, cruel stars whispering in its folds,

21

looked about, around, his lips shuffling, shuttling. "Impressive," he said, finally.

"If you would strip to your waist, please."

"That's a very pretty girl who works for you."

"Yes... that's my secretary."

"Really! So hard to find a good secretary now. All the women are working the men's jobs. Where did you find yours?"

"Family."

"Interesting. They told me you were the best stomach doctor in Paris."

"I don't know about 'the best.'"

"Oh?"

"The only one willing to take risks, however: that I am."

"Really?" said the major. He took off his cap. Instantly his expression changed. Nearly bald underneath the cap, loose hairs floated over a painfully narrow scalp, beads of sweat dotted on his head glistened. He looked up. "Can you have the girl help me take off my clothes?"

"I... think she's busy."

"It won't take two minutes and it would make me very happy."

Emile stared at the SS officer. The cruel mouth had slipped into a smile—a thin, sharp smile.

Emile touched his hands to his chest. "Just a moment," he said, cautiously.

"Simone... he wants you to undress him."

"*What?!*" she said, so loudly he was sure the officer could hear from the next room.

"Simone, please," he whispered. "It's an SS."

"I don't want to," she said, so uncomfortably loudly that the word RESIST seemed to have been plastered all over the flat, over every wall of the office, in every wrinkle of every face.

"Mein Herr... she is very busy," said Emile, reintroducing himself into his office.

"I'll wait," said the officer.

"Just a moment," said Emile again, turning toward the door, stopping himself in mid-step, turning toward the major, who still sat gleaming, whispers of sweat drops streaming in rivulets on either side of his face.

"Yes, Doctor?"

"I am not sure if I can keep my patients waiting. *I* will wait, of course, but it seems... unfair to..."

"You mean to that *priest*? That priest can pray to God. God will help priests—won't He?"

"Major... I... er... Simone? *Simone?*"

She stuck her head in the door. *"Yes, Doctor?"*

"Would you explain to the major why you cannot always help take off the shirt of each patient?"

She looked at the major with the same "Bonjour, mein Herr" smile she had worn a minute ago and said, "Well, I *am* busy. Quite, quite busy, Major—you would be surprised." She stared at him.

In that stare there was something like appeal for all the French trampled, sliced up, shot, deported, tortured; something of quarter asked for an entire country; something, too, of forgiveness of whatever personal wrongs the major might have committed, with his worried scalp, his folded-up, beastly stomach; something inviting....

"Mademoiselle," said the major, as Frenchily as he could, "would you *please* help me... remove my coat, shirt, and tie... for the purposes of this examination?"

"Gladly," said she. Emile watched as if in slow motion she advanced to meet him, to touch him, in the merciless glare of the reflective upside-down stainless-steel bowl filled with light bulbs; watched, trying to look at anything else, as she with expert fingers unbuttoned every silver button, with perfect precision loosened his tie, undoing the knot with a dramatic swish, exactly, but exactly, as she undressed him, Emile, in *their* room at night.

He watched with something like horror as her well-practiced, knowledgeable fingers raced over every white button, while commenting on "what a lot of decorations you have!"

"Yes—for combat, too."

"I hope you didn't kill too many Frenchmen," she said, pouting, folding the jacket delicately, with perfect knowledge of where a man's jacket folds, laying it with almost-love on the chair's back. The back of the chair faced Emile.

"I didn't kill any," he said.

"Oh, I'm so gl—"

"Not personally," he finished his sentence.

She finished winding the tie into a neat roll, so he would be able to whip it open, while considering him and his revolver-trained fingers, his battle-stained clavicle. *Something* had happened there.

Now for the shirt. Emile turned his back. But there was a round mirror on the desk before him, and he watched the fingers glide from button to button, unfastening, the red lips of his female held in a kind of pink resolve as she undid each stitch of the Waffen-SS shirt.

"Raise your arms," she said, standing behind him, considering his hard, bronzed neck, and the officer gently raised his arms, spread apart, slightly behind him, while Emile watched him in the tiny convex mirror, watched the dull echo of a religious scene: Christ in a loincloth, arms spread and crucified; Mary Magdalene.... His pulse pounded and he became aware of ferocious hatred and envy for this man's power—his power over his girl, over *him*—this subtle black cunning; Emile's anger frothed in him like a slow-motion bomb, liquid drying in the throat.

"That's enough," he said, more loudly than he intended.

"What's that, Doctor?" said the major, smiling, happy, good-humored; his teeth were very white.

"Ah? Oh. Er... I'm thinking." He seized a pen and stabbed the tip to the paper.

"Thank you, mademoiselle," said the major, now bare-chested.

"It is nothing, mein Herr. Oh! Is that the telephone? Excuse me."

25

Emile continued staring down at his piece of paper, staring, staring, staring. What was he going to say, to do, to this metal brute, this warrior made of German skin?

"Well... what do you suffer from?"

"French food."

"We did not *ask* you to come here," said Emile coldly.

"And I was *not* being serious," said the major, his face reverting to its pallor, his great bulb of a head reflecting light as if covered with dewdrops.

"Yes, yes, I see."

The major glared beneath Teuton brows, slid his eyes in his sockets, like machine guns in gun emplacements, and said, "Is she your mistress... Doctor?"

Emile stood in place. He had turned around, and together they seemed like two statues, a moment of waiting captured in bronze in city light: Emile in his white coat, notepad held in hand, looking over solid, impenetrable glasses toward the major, sitting, hands by his sides, bare-chested, vulnerable.

Finally, like a tank turret, Emile rotated his head in its socket. He said nothing.

"Doctor... shall we proceed with the examination?"

Emile kept turned away.

"My stomach hurts. It hurts especially after I eat. And my stools are rather painful to pass! I get exercise, you can imagine, and I eat the best food Paris can provide."

"That food's not what it was."

"Of course, I understand. Still... it hurts. Our military doctors cannot determine what is wrong. Of course, our *best* doctors are at the front."

"Eradicating stomach disorders. I knew I had much to fear from the Reich." Emile coughed—a sort of theatrical *kefkefkef.* "Well, Major—since you must choose between guns and butter, and are determined to conquer France, we must cut short the butter, musn't we? And the inner lubrication will suffer."

"We have plenty of lubrication. But even SS cannot drink motor oil."

"I don't recommend motor oil."

"What then *do* you recommend? A brothel? Armistice?"

Emile glared at this. "Who recommended me to you?"

"That is not your concern. Why do you care to know? My connections are irrelevant.... Oh, why not? The chief doctor at the College of Medicine."

"*Him?* He's joking. He means to electrocute you. Through me."

"Try. Have you ever killed anyone?"

"I was a soldier, in '14. A surgeon. I was issued a pistol—which I fired many times. As an act of mercy."

"Mercy? *Mercy?* Mercy killing?"

"Duty, Major. To relieve suffering."

"The *merciful* doctor?"

"I lost a brother, Major. To a *German* bomb."

"And I have lost a son, to German ideas.

27

Don't look so surprised. Why are you surprised? It's very natural. My son was pure Aryan, but... he fell in love. He married. A Jewess, regrettably. He converted. You can imagine what happened next. I am a sworn officer. Yes? I have my duty. They vanished together. My only son. My wife, regrettably, is still alive. Shaking her head in Berlin—never approved of the match, she says, she keeps saying. She blames me, for not having stopped it—curiously approves of what happened afterward. Who would have thought things would get so *very* bad? So very awful, so *soon*? Now that I think about it, my stomach began to hurt soon after they vanished. Hmm. Do you suppose it's psychological? Doctor?"

"Perhaps. Possibly. Might be. An ulcer is often, in a sense, psychological."

"You mean imaginary?"

"Not imaginary—no. Disease—a disorder—can be caused by emotions, and yet produce a real, physical illness."

"Fascinating. Do you see more psychological illness since the war began?"

"No, I see less. Perhaps if one's stomach is blown off it has less time to send imaginary messages." He turned to his patient. "I wonder, mein Herr, if you will take a few deep breaths and relax? I am going to listen to your heart, just as a routine."

"I have a good heart," replied the Major.

"Yes, well, you must allow *me* to judge that."

The major smiled. "Of course, Doctor."

28

Emile took up the stethoscope from its drawer and placed the two listeners, like the tongs of an obstetric forceps, into his ears, and with his right hand he guided and slid the shiny disk across the major's hairy chest. The hairs seemed to envelop, touch, almost caress the doctor's fingers; and the doctor's fingers, gingerly, cautiously, as if probing a minefield, pressed here and there; and his face, averted towards the window, nonetheless came so close to touching the major's face; and he, smiling, looking down at the fingers, conscious of the loving care of this doctor, the attention, the gentleness.

"Your heart is normal," pronounced Emile, drawing back with speed and stiffness. "Now I must examine your stomach. In my experience men prefer to be examined while they are sitting. Women prefer to lie down. Do *you* have a preferred position, mein Herr?"

The major smiled lightly. "You will not find me unusual."

"Very well."

Fingers: kind, probing fingers, palpated, pressed against the tummy of the major, a little pressure here, there—"Does it hurt here?" "Ja." "Here?" "Nein." "Here?" "A little." "Here?" "A lot. Yes yes yes—there."

Then, for the next part of the examination, Emile had the officer lie down on his back, with his head dangling over one side of the examination bed; he asked the major to open his mouth, and shone a lamp down the esophagus.

"Swallow, please."

Peristaltic waves rippled down the pink tunnel.

"Very good. You may sit up." Emile took a few notes in his pad, furrowed his blond-and-white brows, set his mouth hard. He looked at his patient with scientific detachment. "You are bleeding, Major, inside. Your stomach is slowly digesting itself. It's very bad, Major; you may want to consider surgery."

"Really? A man can function with a hole in his stomach?"

"You can function with a bleeding finger, can't you? You can even pull a trigger with a bleeding finger. You can execute someone with a bleeding finger. But it's not recommended."

"Is surgery expensive?"

"Won't Reich doctors do it for free?"

"I can't trust Reich doctors."

Emile's eyebrows darted upwards in a Gallic shrug of the face. "You are taking on the manners of the natives. Whom *will* you trust?"

"No one."

"I think this ulcer is affecting your brain, Major. Shall I give you the instruments? You can operate on yourself, then."

"No, I don't trust myself, either."

"Irony? In an SS?"

"No. You're deluded."

"Very well, Major. I will do it. Do you have money?"

"Of course, Doctor."

"But I desire *American* dollars."

"Insane."

"I have faith in those neo-Germans."

"Not a chance."

"If American dollars are too difficult, psychologically... you can pay me with gold."

"Marks—why not Marks?"

"Why not dollars?"

"Don't ask me to raise the currency of the enemy."

"Gold, then."

The two men looked at each other.

"You must be a Jew, to press such a hard bargain."

"Realistic Christian, mein Herr."

"Christian? Really? We imagined you were all gone."

"No... we have merely become cleverer."

"You are quite extraordinary, Doctor, to be talking to me this way. If Churchill and Roosevelt weren't cousins, and if we hadn't been so cavalier with Roosevelt's real country, the Axis would be mighty. But America? Trust me, they are only out for their wallets. Their women want your lipstick and not our tanks in New York. A unified Europe is a better business deal. 'The business of America is business'? They are our cousins, our families, our prodigal sons. They will not let us fail."

Emile hadn't even shifted an eyebrow. "Forty grams," he said, quietly. "Of gold," he added.

"Thirty."

"Thirty-five, Major."

"Thirty."

Emile hesitated. "Thirty, then."

"And the girl."

"The girl is not bargainable."

"I am not bargaining. She will help me dress. And undress."

Emile started, stared, and strode out of the room. "Simone," he called loudly, "help the major put on his coat. Schedule an appointment for a surgery for him next week. Help him dress. And *stop smiling,*" he hissed.

"Emile?" she queried, as he walked out, back to the waiting room. "Oh la la! How pleasant we feel today, eh? Emile?" When he didn't answer, she clapped her hands down on the desk. "Oh, really! One feels more slave than secretary!" She got up, smoothed the wrinkles from her skirt, stood at the doorway leading to the major, and with a gesture imperious, maternal, and proud, raised the locks in her black hair, unfurled her sexiness like a standard.

"Alors, mein Herr, you have an ulcer."

"Minuscule. All but imperceptible."

"I'm sure you are suffering."

"Bleeding."

"Oah! The doctor will sew you up, good as new."

"Rather an expensive seamstress, wouldn't you say?"

"I am the expensive seamstress, Major. Besides, it's not the sewing but the anesthesia that costs money. Anesthesia, so no more pain."

She was standing behind him, his beautiful all-white cotton shirt with the collar like two knives sticking down. He was raising his arms, behind him, waiting for the hard white ironed cuffs to come over his wrists, slip over him like the first level of mail in an armored suit. Simone pulled the cotton fabric, gently, over the man's arms and the man's muscles, covered smoothly the Nazi flesh, so scarred and so tortured.

"Do you live alone?" the major asked.

"Of course not." She started fastening the buttons of his shirt. Under her tightened skirt the legs curved and invited, and her blouse draped in a translucent white around her neck, her shoulders; she looked down, and the Major saw the strange triangle of the nose seen from above, the curving skin just above the brows, and below, the round, wonderful breasts.

"Do you have a boyfriend?"

"What do you think?"

"Would you like to?"

She had reached the topmost button, the one encircling his neck like a noose. "Don't push your luck," she said, holding on to his sharp collar, holding the two blades of the knives safe. Then kissed him: on the lips, a light peck.

"Your tie," she said, picking up his tie, her fingers flat and hard and reaching far away, as if it were a disgusting sock—even though it was silk. "You don't need *my* help, do you?"

"If you would... please... tie it for me."

"I don't like to tie ties."

33

"Please."

In her hand the full force of the tie unsnapped like a whip. She walked behind him, the two fingers flipping the white collar upwards until it was high and white as an Edwardian ruff. Then the fingers, light, small, the little nails perfectly polished, folded the tie—the rabbit goes around the tree, behind the tree, she was whispering, then down the hole....

He kissed her hand: he stole an area for himself and kissed it, quick as lightning.

"Please!" said she. "You'll make me cross," she added, with mock severity.

"You are irresistible," he said.

"It's only because your wife is very far away."

"My wife doesn't love me."

"Oh, pooh."

"She doesn't. She hates me because I allowed our son to go to a concentration camp."

She handed him the black coat with the silver skulls: the lightning symbols cascading down the crisp fabric, the rows of medals with devices for valor, the wrist cloth with his division sewed in gold.

"You are a killer, mein Herr."

"Only indirectly."

She fastened the five buttons of his uniform, sealing him up in his face as an iron officer. All the hardness returned to his face, what blood he had became mixed with bile, and his mouth came back to cruelty.

"This time next week?" he said, adjusting the cap with the black visor on his head.

"You must not eat or drink anything for twenty-four hours before the operation. Not even water."

"Quite a hard regiment."

"Regi*men*, Major; regi*ment* is what you are in. All right?" She held out her hand.

With almost barbaric menace, and yet with the softest self-control in the world, the major leaned forward, like a machine gun swinging on a pivot, and taking the hand in his, gave it his most heartfelt, longing, lonely, and desiring kiss.

The door opened. Emile and Father Nicolas were standing in it. They traded looks with the Nazi.

"I am saying goodbye," said the major coldly. "Au revoir," he said, and marched out, the heels of his hard boots going click. Click. Click.

CHAPTER THREE

Father Nicolas was invited over for dinner. They hoped to make him seem more human to René, who considered the priest with great fear.

Emile planned the dinner carefully. "Simone, cook lentils. I don't want Father Nicolas watching us eating meat. And just one candle on the table. No need for more."

Simone did as she was told. Emile kept walking round and around the house, looking at everything, especially at his son, whom he'd made dress in patriotic blue-and-white.

Father Nicolas arrived a little late, mumbling about the train schedule and the Nazis at the gates. "They hate us. They hate us because we have claim to a higher authority than they."

He also looked around the house, measuring the preparations and precautions for him. The house was dark, and the candle fluttered feebly; and Father Nicolas suspected that Emile had taken an effort to hide the richness of the house—its woods, its stones, its brass—by lighting nothing.

"This is not the way Marie would have done it," the priest said.

"Yes, Marie would have spent all her money by now. She would have lit everything, burned everything, and you would have eaten a great pile of nothing by a roaring fire."

"Oh, Emile, you're so hard on the poor woman."

"She's much better down there, I assure you."

Father Nicolas answered nothing. He looked at René, whose little legs stuck straight out, like a doll's; his knees were too short to reach the edge of the chair. "When is the boy going to enter catechism?"

"As soon as possible," Emile said. "He needs to be catechized—he needs it badly." The boy sat sullenly at the table, looking at the priest as if at his oldest and most implacable enemy. The priest, by now amused by and accustomed to the hating stares of children, merely smiled. Emile handed him a glass of bitter tea steeped in thyme.

"You could begin catechism now. And be ready in a year. What do you think, René? Do you think you would be ready to receive the body, and the blood, of Our Lord—in one year merely?"

René stared back crossly.

"I very much doubt he will *ever* be ready," Emile said, drinking his tea.

"René only likes games," said Paulette.

"I don't *want* to get confirmed," moaned René, looking down at the house cat, a tabby who sometimes waited for scraps.

"Simone! Get this cat out of here!"

"You must realize," said the priest, lowering his voice to an awful whisper, "denying communion is denying God."

"Sounds good to me," said René.

Slap. René's face turned, stung; red rose to his cheeks; the power of his father's blow had rotated his head in its socket. He turned back to face the table slowly. The priest, sitting opposite, was staring at him, twirling his spoon, smiling.

"A tough one," he said. "But sometimes the worst turn out to be the best."

Paulette was pointing and giggling: "Haa, haa, haa."

"Paulette, don't laugh like that," said Simone, coming in from the kitchen with a big iron bowl of steaming lentils, the fumes rising.

"Ahh," said the priest. "Are we going to have any wine?" he asked hopefully. "To drink?"

"Simone. The priest wants to drink. Bring him something."

"A bottle?"

"That's what wine normally comes in, isn't it?"

She looked at him: which wine? The best? The worst?

But Emile was looking down at the tablecloth, emblazoned MM, the cloth, like the glasses, the silver, part of Marie Marcouire's dowry.

"Bring us a bottle from your vineyard," Father Nicolas said.

"Yes," said Emile. "Bring us one of *her* bottles. That is, one of *ours.*"

She was still down there, among haunted phantom vineyards whose grapes were no longer sweet, in a house where the shadows gobbled the living, in a village where even the water in the fountain stood still. With no car, no money, she could never come up and haunt him in Paris.... He was safe.

"So, Emile: How is Marie?"

Emile's lips twisted. "She keeps herself occupied. Vineyards, animals. Peasants. Horses. Horse races. Et cetera."

"Hmm," said the priest, watching all the liquid rubies drip into his glass. Simone filled all the adult glasses and then said, "Children? Water?"

"Why not give them wine?" asked Father Nicolas.

"There isn't that much wine," Emile said.

"Suffer the little ones..."

"We do!"

"Emile, you old crank."

"I'm an adult," said Paulette. Simone filled her glass.

The adults raised their glasses. "To the end of the war," they said—René lifted his tumbler full of water and stared at everyone jealously. The still-stinging slap felt like pins dragged across his cheeks.

"I don't suppose they let you see her very often," the priest said.

"I've visited her once."

"Of course, of course. Every month?"

"Once."

"You might go more often, no?" Father Nicolas said, turning around, admiring the tablecloth, superbly white, stitched and restitched by a hand in Argelliers, and the glasses, with their fine lines cut in bands of crystal.

"We're not that rich," said Emile.

"Oh, Emile, you old farceur! For a doctor in wartime"—he looked around at luxury, luxury, luxury everywhere—"you're living like a Rothschild. Eh?"

"No. I'm not. Things are tighter than they look."

The priest snickered. "I must take you on your word." But he drank and his face soured.

Emile smiled inwardly. The wine was plonk.

"René." The priest's address—stern, direct—brought René like a trapped mouse to a frenzy of alertness. The boy studied the folds of flesh in the face, the pudgy fingers, the jowls hanging like a dog's. The priest was holding the wine, as if for courage. There was a challenge in beating down, staring, outsmarting little children; and yet to flirt with fear, to risk going too far, was so much part of the fun—it was conquest.

"Are you ready, boy, for the most important day of your life?"

Paulette snatched a piece of bread, flippantly meaning to distract René's attention.

"Answer the priest," said Emile.

"Yes," said René.

" 'Yes, *Father*,' you should say," corrected the priest, gently.

The adults were staring at René, sharp noses above wineglasses, the crucifix behind; Paulette, half adult already, was smirking and chewing a crust of bread, crumbs dribbling all over the tablecloth....

"Answer the priest as he says to answer," said Emile. "He is your father too."

"You're not my father!" René cried, getting up in a rush, catching the embroidered white tablecloth in his belt buckle, and dragging away with him crystal, vases, wine, soup spoons, and soups—all clattering down toward the floor.

"Stop!" cried Emile. But René ran to his room, to safety; and the priest, black under the brows, smiled, raised a finger, while a hand lovingly caressed the crucifix. "Charming," said he.

Emile stood beneath the doorway, glowering. He tightened into a gray rage, then returned in his tight suit to the table, grim, grave, embarrassed.

"Oh, don't worry," said the priest to Emile, fingers descending from the cross on his chest, to the forks and knives, now randomly scattered. "Believe me, I've dealt with much harder children than this one. Much harder. And I've always won. In the end, they believe. They believe Christ was sacrificed for them, died for them. No matter what he believes now, he'll believe Christ loved him, was thinking of him, once I've finished."

"I'm sure he will," said Emile, stealing a glance at Simone, who was staring at the lentils.

Once, when he was a young boy in the Jesuit school, Emile, going down the corridor, had seen two priests in their cassocks, one a monsignor, the other an acolyte, but both in black, the monsignor with the scarlet cap, red as blood. They seemed to lean like old trees.

They spotted him and in three strides were upon him. "What are you doing?" they asked him.

"I am returning—from the doctor. New glasses."

"Show me the glasses."

Emile gave the priests the glasses. Already he was so myopic he was helpless without them. The priest took the glasses, held them up to the light, examined them for dust, for tricks, for truth.

"You'd better not tarry," he said. And without his glasses Emile was only aware of robes, black robes, folds of silk, swish, huge, grown-up feet in cruel black shoes, cassocks swinging, silken cords swinging, like bells....

Dinner resumed after Simone had straightened forks, knives, and soup spoons back to their places on a dampened cloth. Dinner resumed without René.

The priest slurped at his spoon. "Where did you learn to cook, madame? I mean, mademoiselle."

Emile's eyebrows rose on his face in a kind of warning.

"At home," Simone said.

"At home? Where is home?"

"Nanterre." The priest looked at her as if she had still not answered the question. "The *poor* side," she added.

"Ah." Slurp. He turned to the house's master. "You know, Emile, you're very lucky to have found someone like Simone."

"He didn't 'find' me," Simone shot back.

"Oh?" The priest wiped his lips. "Such a fine cook. I'd love to have a cook. A cook—you know—for the kitchen?" He looked around, amused. "But we're not allowed. Alas. Not until cardinalship."

"I'll get more soup," Simone said, face hard. As she got up, the priest watched her ankles, underneath the woolen skirt, a heavy patriotic blue, rustle-swish, rustle-swish.

"We're discussing your secretary. Your cook. Aren't we? That's what I *think* we're discussing. Was I wrong?" And now his brows lifted in such candor, such soft victimization, that his whole body seemed to rise like an El Greco saint from his seat.

Unspoken subjects floated like black flak all over the dinner table; fumes curled and slid over each other in the air until their every eye pointed at Simone. Her shoulders sagged. "Emile, help me," she said. "This is heavy."

"Yes," he grunted, and standing up, nearly ripped off the tablecloth with his belt buckle.

René, hidden behind a pillar on the topmost rung of the stairs, chuckled.

As if some immensely heavy heirloom were being transferred, the bowl changed hands, and Emile brought it to the table.

René sat at the top of the staircase, watching the priest eating lentil soup, knowing it was *his* lentil soup, soup forfeited by not answering "Father."

"My brother was killed... just last week," said the priest. He put down the wineglass.

"Really," said Emile, his fork above his plate, floating.

"Yes," Nicolas gasped, with something like a practiced sob. "Not sure why—Gestapo picked him up. Don't *think* he was part of the Resistance. Still, you see what I have to go through. Cannot complain, cannot confess; I have done nothing wrong."

"My brother was killed at Verdun," said Emile.

"Ah. Ah, ah, ah. Yet—who shall make the pain go away? Who? God. Only God. Only God brings relief."

Thought René: There is no God. Let that Father be buried, or burned, without crosses, without speeches, without smoke or incense or prayer. The earth made him: let the earth have him. And no one can bring relief to me now. Heaven is nowhere: God is no one.

"How is she? Marie?" the priest asked.

"Oh, fine," answered Emile blandly. "She had no brothers to lose."

The priest kept his nose in the soup. "Yes, yes, of course, preserve the estate."

"I mean—to lose at Verdun."

"So sorry—"

"Maman is very happy," said Paulette.

"Oh, is she?" asked the priest, turning with interest and intensity to Paulette.

"Yes, Maman is happy to be among the grapes—the farm, the horses. She doesn't like Paris," she added, squirming her face into a farcical impression of a local snob.

"Doesn't like Paris!" cried the priest, with a squeak.

Again, Paulette shook her head from side to side, balancing scorn and duty. "Never, ever liked it. Papa likes Paris, but only during the week. Simone and I are both practically Parisians."

High in the staircase, hungry, shielded by the banister, René watched the adults laugh and talk without him. Without him, his sister did the Parisian thing, imitating the snotty women, the fast-paced clerks, the haughty aristocrats, to the delight of the adults. Without him, the priest finished his second helping of

44

lentil soup. Without him, Simone held Emile's hand. The priest could not see: he was beyond, on the other side. Paulette could not see. But René saw—saw that hand hold that hand, that hand belonging to another woman by marriage—phantom marriage.

"You are liars!" he cried.

Instantly the illicit hand grasp slipped. Emile turned with ferocious suddenness toward the stairs. "It's that boy."

"Yes," said Father Nicolas, moving in. "Now you must, eh? You must. You want to send him to catechism. Teach him discipline—honor. He'll learn to respect his parents." He wiped his face with a table napkin stitched MM.

"I don't need catechism."

Emile slammed down his glass. "I'm going to beat that boy."

"Emile, don't."

Emile shot her a glance like steel. Their gazes met, sizzled in the air. "He wants punishing. This is the second time this week he's caused a mess and I want to slap him. Teach him."

"Oh, go on then," said Simone. The priest smiled at her appreciatively.

"Sometimes you *have* to be hard. Love *must* be hard. Otherwise, they never learn, and the world teaches them instead of you, and it hurts them for it...." Blandly, talking in oily words gliding from his moist mouth, the priest told her about the sword sent down by Christ to the priests and administered in small, razorlike doses to the children—

SLASH!

From upstairs came a crack and whimpering. A leather belt had smashed skin: upstairs, a boy was being beaten—

SLASH!

Simone looked down at the spots of lentil soup trailing all over the tablecloth, like snail trails, more to wash—hand-wash; the cotton would absorb all the wine. Mounds of salt had been poured over the wine. She looked up at the priest; he was sweating from all the soup; he examined her, examined every line, touched her with his probing eyes, asking questions with the corners of his mouth, unspeakable questions with nothing but his eyes—

SLASH!

Wailing and crying began upstairs. Paulette listened with a discreet, cruel smile—red hair pretty against her white skin. Girlishly, she sat with her knees on her chair.

"Paulette, don't sit with your knees on your chair," chided Simone.

"Yes, don't. Don't do what your mother tells you not to. Don't."

PART TWO

Two Years Earlier—1942

CHAPTER FOUR

René had his ear pressed to the door. The keyhole was almost big enough for a child's finger; just big enough to contain a whole person when she stood on the other end of the room.

Simone lifted the cigarette to her lips and looked in the mirror in the bedroom. She smoked nowhere else. "Even if you gave it to her, it's yours. She can't deny it to you."

Emile was sitting near the door, behind it, so that René couldn't see him. "I know," Emile said. "But it seems wrong somehow."

Simone looked down and looked sad. "It will be wrong if all of it goes to the races."

"It won't. She's not that stupid."

Simone took a deep breath, and the smoke flickered inside her nostrils, came out in waves of compassionate strategy.

"Psst!" It was Paulette, creeping out of her room in her nightdress.

René put a finger to his mouth, demanding quiet. He peeked back at the keyhole, through which light filtered as if at a peep show.

"What's going on?" Paulette whispered.

"They're talking about Mommy," René whispered. "Quiet!"

Simone said, "I could help you."

"No... it's really too risky. She doesn't know."

"Of *course* she knows, Emile; how could she *not* know?"

"I don't think she does. She's not Parisian; she doesn't jump to conclusions like that. If I tell her it is so, she believes it."

Simone blew out more smoke, shapes of dragons, lobsters, things with claws that bite.

"I wonder... send Paulette?"

"What??" whispered Paulette. "Let me see!"

"Shut up!" said René. He pushed her down, squashed her almost destructive curiosity with a hand, and held his ground.

"Is she old enough?"

"She's old enough to know. Old enough to— Is that someone at the door?"

"Only the wind."

Simone walked toward the door. Like birds scattering, the children ran to their rooms, jumped under covers, and pulled blankets tight.

"Children?" Simone asked, entering the hall. She crossed the hall, still in her heels, and knocked—*toc toc toc*—on the children's room. René and Paulette seemed fast asleep.

"Children?" she asked the apparently snoring bodies. Then she closed the door.

René was up first, at her door almost as soon as she closed it. Paulette, less daring, came up again next to the keyhole.

"They're sleeping," Simone said.

"Both of them?"

"Fast asleep."

"Good. Well, I've decided. Give me a cigarette." The children, outside in the cold hall, heard the almost sexual bat-squeak of

50

the fire being lit close to their father's face, the silence that accompanies the first puff. "I'll go with Paulette. I'll tell Marie I'm going to drop Paulette off. I'll have to get a pass for both of us."

"What about René?"

"Oh, take him to the circus or something."

"There is no circus."

"I don't care what you do with him."

René started. Simone looked bitterly pleased, legs crossed, still standing in the doorway. Years later, my father would understand the power she possessed between her legs, power that caused Emile to leave his wife all but confined to a farm in Argelliers—although she liked the confinement of her land, her acidic grapes, her sour old age; she was born on the vine and would die on it.

"When?"

"I'll get the pass for this weekend, if I can. I know the prefect; he's a friend of Nicolas's; he might speed things along."

"What a lot of people you know, Emile."

"What a lot of a people I *don't* know."

She had crossed the room and was now invisible to the children. René twisted his head far to the left, looking through layers of lock through a progressively tighter and tighter keyhole until the sliver of light was trapped by the dark. Paulette shoved him aside. "They're kissing!" she said, in what she thought was a whisper.

"The children!" exclaimed Emile.

They scampered with the baby thunder of

mini-elephants across their hall and into their room. Paulette made the mistake of slamming their door shut.

"Oh, that's *it*!" said Emile. He opened the door and strode into the hall, his adult footsteps dark and muffled in his slippers.

"Emile, your cigarette—don't leave it burning on the dresser!"

"All right, get up, both of you!" Emile said, bursting into their room.

"Emile!"

"Get up, both of you!"

"Hmmm?" said René, stirring as if awakened from Brünnhilde's sleep.

"All right, if you don't get up at the count of three, things are going to get cracking. One!"

"Emile!" Simone shouted. She hissed at him hysterically. "For God's sake," she said in a stage whisper, "if you act as if it was a big deal they'll think it was a big deal! Don't be an idiot!"

"What? Oh? Ah..." Emile, confused, stammered, said, "Umm... good night, children."

And closed the door. In the dark, Paulette and René flicked their eyes open and listened as intently as spies to the footsteps receding— the heavy footsteps of their father and the light footsteps behind. Only René heard the soft, dignified farmer's tread, a pair of phantom feet, far down in Argelliers.

Emile had no trouble getting the passes. He had twice lent the prefect his car, and before the war they had often seen each other in their favorite restaurants.

"Children," he announced at dinnertime a few days after. "I have a proposition to make you. I have two passes with which we can visit Maman Marie."

Simone stirred the soup, looking down at the bubbling liquid.

"I will drive you, but, alas, I cannot stay. So my pass is only for one day. The other pass is for a week. Next month I will get two more passes. Paulette, since you are the eldest, you can go first."

"Noooo!" René moaned.

"Re*né*..." Emile lifted the end of his name ominously. "No complaining. She's the eldest."

"She's *always* the eldest."

"Yes, so she *always* goes first."

"Awww!"

"Re*né*..." said Emile again, again raising the end of his voice like a whip.

René fell into silence.

"I will drive Paulette and leave her among the hayseeds."

"The vineyard," René corrected.

"The hayseeds. Then, a week later, I will obtain another pass to drive her back up. Or she will take the train."

"Yes!" cried Paulette. "I'd love to take the train."

"It all depends on how nice the Nazis want to be. Since everyone wants to get out of Paris during the summertime, I expect they'll be particularly ungenerous. What a pity France is on her knees. Frailty, thy name is woman."

"Emile..." admonished Simone.

"Oh, God damn it, it's not my fault I'm not a Pétainiste."

"It's not that. The walls have ears."

Emile looked at his two children. "They had better not." He readjusted his spectacles on his nose. "Twenty years they spend building the bloody Maginot Line, and the *Boches fly* over it. Bravo, France." He looked at both his two children. "Why didn't I give you German lessons? They always spare interpreters. But why bother? This country will *always* be at war." He looked down at the table, saw his brother struggling along the top of a trench, bearing a body, when *whooooooo-BLAM!!!* Mortar shell in the gut. Half of him blown away. Emile got there in time for the death throes, for the last syllables spoken in the universe, the final valediction; Emile had written it down, had always kept those ultimate words inside his wallet, like a saint's medallion....

"Always war in France. Always with the Germans. Always, people never get along. 'And for a patch of land that hath no worth in't but the name....' " Emile looked at receding smoke clouds, the thousands upon thousands of bodies he had seen as an army doctor; hopeless cases; he had shot many men who had begged him to kill them; he had administered amputations, without anesthetic, with nothing more than a few mouthfuls of *pinard* to calm the nerves; he had blood on his hands. French blood, French youths cut in half like blades of grass in front of Kraut machine-gun fire, youths with their knees blasted away; youths with their arms torn up and shredded, youths praying, the chaplains overwhelmed with the blood, the blindness, the maiming, the suffering.... He looked at his children, at his son. Why had he not gotten them out earlier? The medical practice; but no one had expected that Paris would fall in *six weeks....*

"Weak country," he repeated to himself.

"The train," said Paulette, as if to bring Papa out of his reverie.

"The train? No... he died on a stretcher... at the field hospital...."

"Papa? Are you there?" asked Paulette.

"Eh? Oh! Oh, I—"

"The train!" said Paulette.

"Oh yes, the train. You may take the train up... if Fritz decides not to let me pass the lines again."

"I think I'm old enough to take the train alone."

"Yes, you'll travel first-class if you can...."

"Hurray!"

"What about me?" said René, fiercely watching Simone stir the soup. She flicked her eyes at him.

"We're going to go to the Champ-de-Mars."

"I've already been there! I want to go see Maman!"

"You'll go next month," said Emile.

"I want to go now!"

"Oh, for God's sake, don't be so impossible!

Simone," he said, "what am I to do with him? Tell him... propose to him something he will like."

"René, would you like to go see the theater?"

"No!"

"This boy will be the death of me," said Emile, getting up heavily and dragging himself away from the table. "Remember, Paulette, you have to pack for a week. And... well, I'll tell you the rest later."

"Tell me now!"

But Emile would tell her or René nothing.

Paulette packed slowly and cruelly, savoring every moment over René. She said how much she looked forward to all the warm sun at Argelliers, to all that time spent with Maman, showing him each and every item she would pack, explaining what it was for. Finally, one night, watching her, René could bear it no longer, and on his bed, in full view of her, began to cry.

"René! What's the matter?"

"It's not fair," said René. "I love her more than you do."

Paulette's brows came together and knitted with concern. "Ohhh," she resonated sympathetically.

René still cried. "It's not fair. Maman loves me more *too*."

"You'll get to go next week."

"You mean next *month*! I'll probably *never* be able to go."

"René—would you like to go in my place?"

René was so startled his tears stopped as if

a faucet had been cranked shut. "You—really will let me go?"

"If Papa will let you, and if it means so much, yes."

"Oh, Paulette!" The squall of tears faded and it was summertime in his eyes again. He leapt off the bed and cried, "I have to tell Dad!"

"Not *now*, you idiot!" hissed his sister. "Wait till morning!"

But René would not wait. He went straight to his parents' bedroom, knocked on the door, and walked straight in.

Emile had his head hunched, a sidewise angle, and his eyes had been closed, yet seeing things, close to Simone, their faces touching, their lips touching. They came apart as if a wind had knocked apart two apples on a tree.

"René!" cried Emile. His father looked at him angrily, real confusion over his face.

"Paulette says she'll let me go see Maman this week and she'll go next month! I want to go!"

René saw the massive black shape of his father approach in the bedroom—the slacks full of manhood, darkening, approaching like a storm. Emile looked straight down at his puny son, his whitening brows sheltering two pools of blue heat.

Father and son stared at each other in that interrupted intimacy.

"You can't," said Emile.

"Why not?" said René, his desire to see his mother overpowering all fear of his father.

"Because I said so."

"Why not?! Paulette says she'll *let* me go. It's not fair! Just because *you* don't love Mommy doesn't mean that *I* don't!"

Time froze—the smoke from Simone's cigarette rose, curled once about the room, turned and crossed its arms, pouting at René. All the wooden furniture seemed to tick like bombs.

"Simone..." groaned Emile. "Explain. Tell him. Tell him anything."

"René, you are being *very* unreasonable. You're not being realistic—what do you want me to tell you?"

"I'm *not* being unreasonable. Paulette said she would *let me go*!!!"

"René, listen. The tickets... were made out in the names of your father and of Paulette."

"I can change them! Let me see them! I'll change them."

"*No*, you don't understand. Go to your room and stop complaining."

"*No*."

Emile looked at him in the savage darkness accumulating around them. He unbuckled his belt, and the fine leather snapping through the buckles as he unfurled its full hard length sounded like a train crossing tracks. Emile spoke. "Go to your room. Or I'll whip you."

René watched, looked, felt the fear rise in him like a drowning liquid. Looked at his father, standing with a coil of leather like a cobra's head, arched, ready; and Simone, her smoke curling around her and around the room.

René started to cry, right there, right then. At a wave from the belt he ran from the room, buried his face in the pillow, and wept and sobbed—for his mother, all that time without his mother, Nazis round his mother, Nazis round Paris, this entire year ruined because of the adults and their damn wars that he didn't even understand.

"I told you—you should have waited until morning," said Paulette.

On the morning of the departure, Emile took out his Chenard-Walker, lifted the great hood, inspected the plugs, stuck his big nose in the radiator, squinted at the fan belt, peered, went round the car, looked carefully at the tires, frowned, cursed and muttered under his breath, decided to change a tire, jacked it up, got it off, ran his fingers along the treads, sniffed at it as if at a pot-au-feu, decided to put it on again, jacked the car down. He was ready to go.

Paulette had taken enough suitcases for two persons. Emile hardly noticed. "You have everything?" he asked her, and she might have taken the question literally.

René stood around, sad as a rainy day. Simone tried to get behind him and lower a maternalish hand on his shoulder, but René grimaced and shook it off as if it were a fly. Simone relented and let the boy stand alone.

"I'll be back before two," Emile said, as the great engine rumbled to life. He meant two in the morning. Since he didn't wish to see his wife, he would arrive, drop Paulette off, and return.

"You're sure Rainbow is running today?" asked Simone, almost teasingly.

"Yes, yes," Emile replied, mentally lowering driving goggles over his eyes. The Chenard had a perfectly serviceable windshield, but Emile had removed the roof. "It was her favorite, a year ago. Nothing will have changed."

Now Emile gunned the engine, and smooth as an airplane the machine glided down the tarmac and then vanished out of sight.

René was inconsolable. Simone said, "René, you mustn't pout."

René pouted.

"You mustn't sulk."

René sulked.

"You really mustn't *dwell* on it."

René dwelled on it, made a house on it, moved mentally into it.

"Do you want to see a show?"

"No."

"Do you want an ice cream? On the Ile Saint-Louis?"

"No."

"Do you want—"

"I want to see my mommy!!!" René cried, almost bawling.

"Dear, dear—am I so awful?"

"I hate you," René said, with total finality.

"Well, then," Simone said, with practiced dismay, "we must find ways soon to be rid of each other."

"Yes... you don't belong with my father."

"That's not what your father thinks."

"My father married Mommy. He didn't marry you."

Simone took a deep, deep breath, saw the Catholic Church rising before her, all its splendid saints, bleeding, upside-down crucified, all its women, its virgins and sluts, its sexlessness. Nothing for an atheist.

She walked along, in her elegant black dress, her curvy legs rising underneath her skirt, her tightish jacket, every inch the kept woman of the Ninth.

At the border the Chenard-Walker was stopped by a troop of Frenchmen. The corporal who greeted them after they had waited in a queue of five other cars was bonhomial, even jovial.

"*Liberté, égalité, vos papiers,*" he said, with a khaki smile full of brown teeth.

"Ah, you're getting a sense of humor," said Emile.

"Yes, yes, I love humor. Get out of the car."

Emile, confidently reaching through his jacket, through the old French wool, came up with the two passes which he wished to show to the corporal.

"Is this your car?"

"Yes," said Emile, showing the papers to the corporal.

"Do you have registration papers?"

"Yes... they're in the car." Emile made a motion toward the car.

"Hep!" cried the corporal, as if he'd found

a spy. Emile froze leaning into the car, his butt exposed; he heard the leather pitter-patter of feet round him.

"You did not ask permission to get into the car."

"I feel like you're my mother, corporal."

There was a silence as the corporal considered whether this remark might be insolent.

"Get out of the car."

Emile leaned out of the car, keenly aware of the cold gunmetal all around him, the tightly drawn jackets. The corporal was a little shorter than he was and looked him in the eye.

"What do you do?" the corporal asked, looking at his papers.

"Doctor."

"That explains the car. What kind of doctor?"

"Stomach doctor."

"Surgeries?"

"Sometimes."

"Do you treat Germans?"

"Yes."

"Not very patriotic of you, is it?"

"I charge them double."

"Good. Is this your daughter?"

"Yes."

"What's her name?"

"Paulette."

"Paulette? Hello, Paulette. What's the matter—are you afraid to speak to me? Hmm? I'm not going to hurt you. Let me see your papers, please."

Emile gave him the papers. All three stood still as dunes on a desert.

"Motive for visit? Search the car, you others."

"The child is going to visit her mother."

The men in brown entered the Chenard-Walker, opened its compartments, poked its seat cushions.

"The seat cushions are quite rigid, Corporal," said a private.

"Have you got someone under your seat, doctor?"

"No, Corporal. The only things under the seats are the cushions."

"Stab it with a knife, private. Why is your wife not in Paris, Doctor? Do you not get along?"

"She runs our farm."

"Why not run it yourself?"

"We are separated."

"Nothing under the seats, Corporal!"

"Like France.... What's in the luggage, you lot?"

"It's the girl's clothes, Corporal. Lots of lots and lots of clothes."

"How long is she staying down?"

"A week."

"*Lots* of clothes!" a private re-echoed.

"Sounds more like a month. Sounds like she's moving. Are you smuggling her out? Now why would you want to take such a pretty young girl out of Paris? Isn't that where a pretty girl wants to be? Why is she moving?"

"She's not moving."

"Then *why* so many clothes? Eh?"

"Paulette?" her father asked.

"I thought I would need them. You never know."

"You never know what?" asked the corporal, with a gentle sneer.

"What the weather will be like."

"It's going to bake you like an oven and then piss on you like hell. Where did you get the car, Doctor?"

"France."

"But it's English-made."

"Yes... I got a good deal."

"Cheaper than Volkswagen?"

"Undoubtedly, Corporal."

"How's the girl getting back?"

"Train."

"Why not have her take the train now? And spare yourself the trip? You won't have a lot of time to spend with your wife, if you want to be back by two, as it says in your return pass. Particularly the way that thing drives, hmmm?"

"I wanted to get out of Paris. Little vacation."

"I am suspicious of little vacations, particularly if you'll be driving every hour. Do you understand? I am suspicious."

"I wish to see the farm."

"But not see your wife. I am suspicious. Maybe you wish to see someone else?"

Emile made no answer.

"Answer, please."

"Yes."

"Inspection finished, Corporal!"

"Well, well, well, Doctor. I hope you have a jolly time in Argelliers." The corporal stuffed the papers into Emile's vest pocket. "I'll probably not see you when you come back tonight. But you'll meet my sergeant friend. He's very friendly, just like me. You'll see."

"Yes, Corporal. Am I dismissed?"

The corporal smiled, leaned away, and the engine roared to life.

Driving away, neither father nor daughter spoke to each other until they were almost halfway across France. Then, Emile began speaking.

"When we get there, I want you to give me a little help."

Paulette merely stared at the miles of French road unrolling.

"I would have brought René, but I'm not sure he's old enough. You're old enough, aren't you?"

"I'm not sure what I'm old enough *for*," said Paulette.

"You'll see."

The hotel was a room above a restaurant. Emile insisted Paulette bring her crates into the bedroom, and wearily ordered that ratatouille be brought to his room, along with half a bottle of red.

The wine was awful. Emile sighed with disgust; he drank it anyway.

Paulette had never slept in the same room with her father, and she watched him surreptitiously—his old, gray hairs, his skinny shanks—and when he got into his bed and turned away from her, he gruffly reminded her they would be up terribly early, and without saying good night, started to snore.

They arrived around noon. Argelliers was sleeping in its bath of sunshine. Shutters were shut for the weekend; Emile knew at nearby Béziers, horses were running and being watched and being bet on.

He pulled into the road that led to the vines. The house rose out of the ground. Earth-colored, with a garden indistinguishably fading into vines, shrubbery rubbing shoulders with grapes, all rising, rising out of earth. He parked the Chenard-Walker in front of the house. "Get out," he said.

He looked around; the insects chirruped and rubbed their wings and legs; the sun beat, casting shadows that wove and unwove worm-like shapes beneath the vines, rotating and squirming slowly as the sun moved.

Emile crossed the courtyard. A horse neighed with curiosity.

The cobblestones glowed with heat; Emile felt the warmth penetrate the soles of his shoes, burn down the wool in his coat, coax the first beads of sweat from his brow. Panting, panting—the whole countryside seemed waiting like a dog in a doorway.

Emile opened the door of the garage. "Come here, Paulette," he called.

"I'm going to put my bags in the house," she said.

"There's no time for that now," he said. "Come here."

The smell from the stable came over him like

66

a cool blanket, the hay mixed with the excrement of horses. He went over to where they kept the farm tools, the scythes, the sickles in their splendid arrays, their long, leaning blades; the pickaxes, the shovels, the spades....

Emile took some of them in his hand, felt their slightly rotten wood, got a feel for their heft, toted the heavier ones in his arms... and picked the pickax.

He slipped off his jacket, already showing circles of sweat round his armpits. "Here, take this. Put it in the car. That damned guard slowed us down. We haven't got much time. She'll be back any minute."

"Time for what?"

"Come here."

Before the back door, he fumbled with the keys, hanging on the special chain marked MAISON. "How unlike her to lock it. Must be the war...."

The door gave and groaned as if unwillingly releasing the secret of the house.

A smell, like old licorice matured in walnuts, or something like the moist pungent smell that emerges from the top of an ancient wine bottle when uncorked, invited them closer. Dusty shadows played everywhere in the house, as playful as cats, and as they walked their steps creaked.

"Follow me," said Emile, hefting the pickax, in shirtsleeves, walking through the dining room, crystal laid out in singing combinations, a decanter full of wine awaiting the lady and her supper....

They arrived at the kitchen. Underfoot was a blue-and-white pattern, a mosaic of porcelainlike squares, somewhat clumsily mortared in a square between the potbelly stove and what served as the sink. A giant cistern mounted above, connected by patchwork tubing to a faucet on the side of the house, bubbled and gurgled nervously.

"We may not need this," said Emile, dropping to his knees and holding the pickax alongside his body, like a mine sweeper and his tool. He seemed to smell the earth. Far away, a dog barked with nervous interest.

Emile stuck his nails into the mortar and plaster. "Damn! It's sealed up tight! Shit!"

He was sweating inside that cool house; far off, the grandfather clock whirred gently and then began chiming.

It was a delicate song, yet earthy, like a peasant singing. Weights and levers whirred and spun in their circles, little precise chains dropped a half-centimeter, sang, and then the clock was still.

"All right—the pickax." Emile stood up, balanced on two feet, looked around for clearance, lifted and then brought down the ax hard.

Striking it rended blue-and-white tile; beneath him the ground collapsed like the false bottom of a suitcase. He fell down to his knees again, panting, sweating, and with his hands dug out clumps of sod, bits of ceramic smashed.

In the ground, underneath a protective barrier made of wood, encased in a brown paper already moldy and weakened with the worming of the earth, lay, in neatly stacked rows, twenty ingots of solid gold.

"Hurry." He lifted one—so heavy!—"Put it, hide it! No one must see it."

He himself took two ingots, one in each hand; Paulette could only carry one with both. They walked out of the kitchen, leaving the gaping wound in the ground like a temple desecrated; he stepped into the blinding, incriminating sunlight and dashed over to the car, which he'd parked next to the back door.

"Bring the rest of them. Quickly!" From the boot of the car he got out the jack: and quickly, quickly, he leaned the jack into the car and began cranking as fast as he could. Rivers of sweat ran. Finally, with the big, custom-made screwdriver, he removed the wheel and got out the spare.

It had been made to look like a spare. He had razored out the lining, reinforced the rubber, and now, instead of air, it was to hold the two kilograms of gold.

Paulette had brought out several of the ingots, and now Emile feverishly tried working them into the tire. He was not sure it would work... it had to work. Cursing, grumbling, yelling "Shit!" and "Christ!" and "Mother of Mary!" under the spit of his breath, he managed to half push, half pull the ingots into places all along the inside of the wheel, in time to go get more ingots, until they were glittering in their places in their hiding hole, while the house mourned.

"Where did you put my jacket?!" he cried.

"It's in the car, Daddy," said Paulette, standing between the hole knocked in the kitchen, the wound in the tire, under the sun beating, beating down.

"Go inside the house. Clean it up. Make it look as if we weren't there."

Paulette stood stupefied.

"GO, I said!!"

Paulette left, bursting into tears, wondering why was it that she and not René had been sent down to do this deed; and she came to the kitchen, picked up the pickax with both hands—too big for her, it would have been impossible for René— and started lugging it toward the shed. Along the way she heard the engine crank, groan, and finally scream to life.

"Papa?" she cried, running to where the car was parked but with its engine rolling, rolling.

"Clean it up, I said! Make it look like before!" And now fierce concentration on what was happening in the tire as the car made its first tentative steps forward.

There was a groan: Emile squinted, pressed his face as if for pain: he got out, as quickly and as fluidly as a nightmare, surveyed the scene—crouched, got on his knees, examined the malignant tire filled to bursting with stolen treasure, decided okay, okay, got back into the car, and crept forward a few feet more. "How's the tire? Eh? Look at it, sister!!"

Paulette stepped forward, her face awash in tears, confusion spreading like an acid over her face.

"LOOK AT IT, I said!!" Paulette dropped to her knees, dirtying her smock, soiling her knees, dirtying the present forever: she touched, gingerly, as a child might touch a womb, the obscenely swollen tire.

"It's fine," she said.

"WHAT?!"

"It's FINE!" she yelled over the Chenard's diabolical whining, and Emile gunned the engine to full life, the tire, gold, swelling, and all, lurched, then moved down the road, then, hitting the highest gear, shot out of sight.

All at once the house resumed its breathing. Paulette heard as if for the first time the awful summertime rhythm of the country—the insects, the birds, the heat rising in waves from the grapes swollen to bursting, their skins taut with the pressure of juices about to explode.

She was still holding the pickax.

Carrying it behind her, as if dragging a corpse, she lugged the passive weapon, almost as big as she was, to the shed, and let it fall among the other half-rotten, half-used weapons of the house. Then she trotted, breathless, hot, and dizzy, the sun blinding her eyes, to the house, to the blue-and-white porcelain-and-glass wound in the kitchen.

The hole where the gold had been: that had to be covered up. In the garden would be clumps of sod, about the right size to fill the hole yawning like a grave. She ran out, thought she saw, far away down the road, old Dolores, the servant woman, coming back, walking from the town—thought she heard a man's whistling in the air. Back to the house, where she interred the sods like so many broken, anonymous soldiers in their common fosse; she tried wrapping the old, moldy paper, as if it still might disguise the metamorphosed contents of the hiding place. The tiles—so many! and so broken! It was like a jigsaw puzzle; she would do the edges first, the largest pieces, the triangular one, this one like a sharp, obtuse triangle, this one like a sliver of a grenade, aimed at a soldier's gut....

"René?" came a call from inside the house. The house shook with the presence of its owner. Paulette froze on her knees on the cold, incriminating kitchen floor. The door unlatched. Steps, old, slow, and shuffling, like an incompetent phantom's footfall, moved, slid, pushed across the house, coming into the kitchen....

"Oh! Paulette. Que fais-tu ici?" Then a cry, the hands raised in terror: "The GOLD! The GOLD!"

Paulette looked up, guilty. Her mother seemed so old, so tired, so worn, so much the *paysanne,* so frumpy, so smelly, bringing the flavor of horses and licorice into the house. Pastis had carved her face with blades of sunshine; her clothes hung about her like old, demented birds. Her legs had become tubular, her eyes glassy, her short, stocky frame bloated by diabetes and water-gathering diseases. Only in her mouth was life—held open for a cry, a spasm of horror, disappointment, help-lessness, rage—treason, treason, treachery.

She took a step forward, slow, like an army, like a chess piece. Moving into position. Her eyes fixed on that gaping wound in the tiles. Another step forward. Another. Paulette pulled back, conscious of the soil on her knees. The dirt. Her hand, dirty.

Maman Marie fell on her knees. On her wrist, a rosary tinkled. Her hands—deeply callused, sharpened and toughened with years of the vines, years of making grapes grow, years of clipping flowers, encouraging the children of the garden, digging here, digging there—came to the broken tiles, like broken glass from a stained-glass window—came to the earth so hastily put back—so unlike the way she had placed it, in the dark, one night when she was sure no one could hear, no one could know, and the one person who did know would never... came to the moist, broken brown paper, torn, desecrated now, removed it with more tenderness that she would touch a baby—and there—instead of the cold, per-petually shining metal, was earth, soil, sod, dirt.

Paulette watched as her mother, kneeling now, clutching clumps of dirt which surren-dered to her fingers, squished with mocking ease, scrabbled through the earth, to see if one ingot, just one had been spared her, but no, they were all gone—all gone.

Paulette watched as her mother began to cry. Paralyzed and overwhelmed, Paulette watched

73

the old, raggedy face crinkle and the blue of her eyes disappear beneath old folds of skin.

For a long time she wept. "Lord," she said. "Lord God." Finally she looked at Paulette, who had scarcely moved, realizing now was the moment why she must prove she and not René had been chosen by her father.

"Is he gone—your father?"

"Back to Paris, Maman."

"God forgive you for what you have done! God forgive you. Oh, how will I survive now? Oh, he didn't dare ask me for them, the coward!" She wept a long time more, brooding over this great hole in her marriage, this absence full of disastrous, foul earth. Paulette thought she had never seen anyone more miserable. Here was a woman who had lost everything but the earth she stood on—lost husband, lost son, lost daughter—no, not lost: *stolen.*

She shook her head: "Traitor, treachery, my child—my gold—gone—and you stand there, pitying your mother! I won't have it! You snotty city kid, so carried away, living off my jewels, and now, what do I get to keep except... shit...."

Paulette would have to stay another week. Dolores came to set her into her room.

"Children, children... at what age are you no longer innocent?" Dolores was old, bent like a witch, and her cheeks flapped like a dog's dewlap. "Why did you do it? Why? What had your poor mother ever done to you?"

Paulette thought of how ugly, how hideous,

this poor peasant woman looked, and a tiny glance at her own white hand was all she needed for support. I am more beautiful than you, she thought. I will always be more beautiful than you.

"You do not answer? Perhaps you have no answer. Aïe aïe, aïe... it's a terrifying time, when the children cut down their parents... or when they gang up on one parent. Why? Why does God send us children like that?"

"Please be careful with my luggage," said Paulette.

Dolores turned and fixed her black eyes on Paulette's black eyes. "Ohhh... we've become the Parisian, have we? We've learned to despise the country folk, have we? Look around, silly girl." Around, the grandfather clock, prouder-looking than the noblest ancestor, stood tall; the marqueterie in the tables, the silver in the mirrors, revolved and shone in the dimmed-down light in the house. "The minute your mother is dead, even while she's still warm, you'll be fighting for this clock, this table, this mirror... you'll be clawing and scratching for your share of the vineyards, and I suspect, proud, insolent little girl, you'll try to turn poor old Dolores away from the house she grew up in, married, buried her husband in, and intends to die in. Oh, yes, wretched girl, we'll see how far your newfound Parisian snobbery takes you when you covet."

"I don't covet anything here."

"Then get out," said Dolores, and dropped

the suitcases on the stairs. "Carry them up yourself," she shot back, and went back down the stairs, to comfort her mistress, still weeping in the kitchen.

Paulette girded her shoulders—she couldn't drag both her heavy suitcases up at once—one at a time, and even then it was a struggle. What work! And who was Dolores to treat her in such a way? She didn't even know until the minute they arrived she was here for theft. All she could do was fall back, as if on a cushion, on her pride. The pride of a Bastien versus that of a Marcouire.

Dinner for mother and daughter began at ten o'clock. Candles were set, wine was set, the silver was set and shone. Maman Marie sat at the head of the table and Paulette off to one side.

"Bonsoir, Maman," she said. They had not seen each other all day. Paulette had shut herself up in her room against the heat; Maman Marie had been out in the fields, tasting the grapes, particularly in *la pépinière,* the sweet spot where the best grapes grew.

"Bonsoir, fille," was the answer. Dolores held out a large porcelain blue basin, into which Maman Marie, having sat down, dipped her hands. In the dining room the sound of water rippled.

Dolores gave a towel to Maman Marie, and she blinked her clear, blue eyes, like a sky at its most intense or like a baby's eyes.

"You don't wash your hands, Paulette?"

"I washed them already, Maman."

Maman Marie's lower lip, thick with wrinkles, stuck out, her eyebrows lifted in skepticism at this strange habit; she looked down at the dinner table, lowered her eyes, clasped her hands, and began saying grace.

In a mixture of patois, and Latin, the shushed and whispering words shuttled across her lips, and it seemed she was calling into existence the very things she was naming: the bread, the charity, the wine, the mercy. Dolores bowed her head and clasped her hands before her respectfully. Maman Marie prayed, prayed for everybody in her strange dialect, the language she reserved for speaking to God; and both Dolores and Paulette were mentioned amidst the invocations, requests, the name of a horse, René, Emile, the health of one of the workers; she asked for countless tender mercies; she named countless people; asked for countless things.

"Amen," she said.

"Amen," repeated Dolores firmly.

"Amen," mumbled Paulette.

"Do you say grace when you're with your father, Paulette?"

"Sometimes."

"He was always more interested in punishment than prayer," said Marie, serving herself the first egg course.

Paulette didn't answer.

"Men," said Dolores.

"What do you think of that, Paulette? Do you think *all* men are more interested in punishment and power than in being humble?"

"I don't know… many men," said Paulette.

"You will, my darling." Marie passed her the egg course.

Dolores kept a savagely watchful eye upon Paulette, as if the impertinent Parisian girl might at any moment try to conceal, steal the porcelain tureen by sticking it into her brassière.

"Dolores, don't stand so close to Paulette," Marie said, adding, "she might bite you. The way you, Paulette, treated Dolores when she was carrying your luggage—shame! Shame, you little thief. This old feeble servant of mine taking your luggage and you have the gall to complain."

Paulette smiled pleasantly. "Your range of expressions, Maman…"

"I have many more, my sweet." A dog came racing into the room. "Toutou!" she said. "Toutou! You remember Paulette? Our Parisian daughter? See if she's good to eat, now. Go on, taste her. Take a nice little bite!"

The dog growled with Alsatian, German, ferocity, baring his fangs at Paulette.

"Oh, he doesn't obey me. Paulette, dear, he doesn't seem to remember you. It's surprising—you're here so often, and you work so hard in the fields."

Dolores snickered. The dog growled.

"Is he always so friendly with family, Maman?"

"He's a good deal friendlier than your father, don't you think? C'mon, Toutou! Maybe you can terrorize Emile and get that gold! But Toutou is very old; I doubt he could finish off even Emile. You're not family,

78

Paulette, even though you like to think you are. My family is standing next to you."

Dolores registered no emotion, but stood with the dignity of an old Greek statue.

"So go on," said Marie. "Tell me what happened. Come here, Toutou! Paulette has to tell a story."

Paulette was quiet.

"So—your Papa decided he wanted to see how his investments were doing?"

Paulette was quiet. The dark dog began to bark.

"Go on," said Maman Marie. "I just want the facts. Toutou, calm down! Later, you can bite her."

Paulette said, "He didn't tell me about the gold until... we were at the house."

" 'Until we were at the house.' " Marie looked at Dolores. "What a swine, eh? He doesn't even tell his daughter until the last possible moment. And then dumps her here. Oh, I've got a fine husband. Go on, my sugarplum."

"Then when we arrived, he parked in the back so you couldn't see the car."

"Yes, on my rhododendrons. Which took Dolores all week to plant. Such a good parking space. Go on."

"Then he went to the tool shed, to get the ax."

"The swine. The cheat. He couldn't even bring his own tools! He uses *my* pickax to dig up *my* gold. 'How often we give our enemy the means of our own destruction,' as Aesop

79

puts it. The poor eagle... That pig! I suppose he filled his car with my gasoline, too! So expensive, gasoline! And so difficult to cash in a solid gold ingot in occupied France! So inconvenient!"

"I don't think he did," cautiously asserted Paulette. "There wasn't time."

"Oh. 'There wasn't time.' Did you hear that, Dolores? 'There wasn't time.' No time to say hello. No time to explain. No time to ask. Listen to this. Listen. I would have given him half of that gold. That was my dowry! *My dowry!* But I, to have latched on justice to necessity, would have parted with that gold as if with my children. Take one—one half was his. And he—he takes it all! Oh, Dolores, why did I agree to marry him? Shall I say it? To please my father. He made the match; it would have slaughtered his bourgeois conscience for his daughter to be a spinster. And now look at me. Is this any better? Are *you* any better? What joy, what confounded *use* have you been to me, Daughter? You're an accomplished thief, and instead of comfort you offer me a bed like a rack. How can I sleep with you in the house? Oh, my father, he tried to be good to the end. And now look at me. This would kill him, to know that your father and I are more at war than troops on the front."

And she cried, softly at first, then louder and louder, wailing like a Gypsy, rising with every sob while the gazpacho waited coldly in its bowl. Paulette sat motionless, watching her mother crying, trying to look like coolness itself, even letting the tiniest and most subtle smile cross her white face.

"Look at this child—absolutely no pity for her poor mother. Absolutely none. Oh, Paulette, you have a lot to learn. Dolores, hold me."

The lady leaned into the servant, who glanced with contempt at Paulette—but with so much eaten-up sadness, even despair, that Paulette felt frozen in her cold place, while Marie sobbed on, sobbed on.

"Dear, dear," Dolores said, patting her lady on the back, with gentle taps, as if it were a child's back, gentle taps. "There, there. Have a bit more soup?"

"Oh, give me some wine."

"No, no wine. Wine be no good."

"Water, then; give me water."

From the transparent decanter, sparkling, active with light, flowed pure freshets of water. Marie drank greedily. "This evening... I went in... I thought it had all been a bad dream. I went in... and looked... and there it was... right in the middle of my kitchen... like a wound, full of dirt. Full of earth. All that gold, gone. Dolores, my handkerchief."

Dolores took out a handkerchief, old, with innumerable blotches, frayed, purple, red, blue, and twisted about (used once as a bandage, as a flag in a flamenco dance, as a chloroform holder in a surgery): she took out that handkerchief and patted her lady's eyes, then held the handkerchief to her lady's nose.

Marie blowing her nose and crying sounded like an enormous braying, the Last Judgment. The room seemed to shake, and there were circles upon circles inside her water glass.

Water inside her glass; water inside her eyes. Water inside the cistern bubbling calmly, letting out one huge bubble every moment like a huge burp.... Dinner went on.

"Come, Paulette. Finish up. I want to show you something."

Paulette finished her fruit compote and cream and drank the last of her wine.

"Dolores, I'm going to show Paulette the upstairs."

"But I've already seen the upstairs," Paulette said.

"Not this room, you haven't."

Marie inclined her head, said grace, and then dislodged herself from the table. Paulette half-mockingly but quickly crossed herself and then followed suit. Marie took one of the oil lamps, turned up its wick so that the flame rose like a white tongue into the spherical orb of glass which contained it, like a round mouth, and burned brighter.

"Come up the stairs, Paulette. Be careful of where you step."

"I've been on these stairs before, Mother."

"Yes, yes, follow me. Your ancestors who built this house built well. There's always a pleasant little draft running through here, as if some spirit were blowing us air to keep us cool. You're quite cool in this house, aren't you, Paulette?"

"I feel quite cool, yes, Maman."

"Good, good." The light had been racing and rushing before them on the staircase, dashing down the hallways like an overeager child impatient to see what was next, what was behind the door.

They had arrived at an old door.

"I normally keep this room locked," said Marie, and she reached into her bosom. "And I have the only key. Even Dolores is not allowed in here."

She opened the door with an effort. It opened with great, immense reluctance, like a stone door on a hinge of stone, or the door of a great tomb.

Scurrying, the light dashed in, illuminated all the walls with half-hearted, fearful light, and ghastly shadows danced around. In the boarded-up darkness Marie's face looked demonic, the light playing beneath her face, the shadows cavorting like black flames, sliding over her face like serpents, the flame flicking in and out like a tongue licking and licking.

Paulette walked in cautiously, and her heart was beating faster.

"I never told how your great-great grand-mother died. The first Marcouire. Do you know where she died?"

Paulette did not answer.

"She died in this room. In this very room, Paulette. Here she decided to blaspheme against God and take her own life. Look up. There is a hook. Upon that hook she attached a rope, and from the other end she made a noose. She asphyxiated, Paulette; she strangled herself, rocking herself backward and forward upon her hook until the air and oxygen and life was burned away and she died with her face blue."

"Why—did she—why did she hang herself?" asked Paulette, trying to toss off the question like a Parisian coin upon the street.

"Because it was when she was late in her forties, and long after she had ceased having relations with her husband, that she realized—she had conceived. She was pregnant with a child. She began to feel the swelling in her body, touching a tumor malignant, feel another life stealing life from her, squeezing her toward death. In her black madness she conceived the delusion that the child was not human—that the child was demonic, diabolical. And she thought the birth of the child would kill her, and that it thereafter would declare war upon her lawful issue. And so— to abort the evil, she seized her life and strangled it.

"People say she haunts this house, but I don't believe that, because I've prayed for her every day, that her soul may rest in peace. And I keep this door shut. But this room is next to your room, Paulette; the wall that divides them is quite flimsy. I would not be surprised if today your great-great-grandmother pays you a visit and recommends you expiate the sin you committed with your father. Oh, yes... oh, yes."

Paulette waited in the silence for a long

time before she nerved herself to say, "I *don't* believe in ghosts."

But she was standing alone in the room when she said it; Maman Marie had already stepped out. Paulette stepped toward the lamp—not fast enough, it seemed to her; the darkness was closing around her like a mouth. Her mother was waiting just outside the door for her, and when Paulette saw her appear as if out of the dark, she started, then immediately tried to regain some cool.

"Now you have seen her room. Now, observe: this is an old-style lock. I'm going to insert the key, and turn it—once. But now I'm going to leave the key in the lock, in case you should want to visit the room tonight."

"I've seen quite enough," said Paulette.

"Oh, well then, I'll leave the key inside in case anyone else wants to get in or out."

Paulette was sleeping ill. Even though she was exhausted from the trip, she was not used to eating so much so late. She was sleeping, and waking, not knowing which was which; slipping in and out of sleep as easily as the shadows had slipped in and out of that room. Paulette figured that her bed was against the wall that joined the other room. It figured, she thought; it's a scare tactic; it was all done on purpose; I bet no one ever did anything in that room except hang up their coat. I bet you there was never even a great-great-grandmother.

There was a knock on the door. Paulette froze. "Yes?" she whispered.

"It's Dolores," a voice said, although it seemed to come from much farther away than the door—to come from—from the other side of the wall. "Come in," Paulette said.

But no one came in. Angrily, in a flush of rage at this cheap trickery, she stormed up, wearing her nightdress, and flung open the door.

No one was there.

Still angrier, Paulette glanced toward the left, where the sinister door was supposed to be. All the light had been extinguished, but she tiptoed down the hall to where she knew the door was, running her hand along the molding. She was looking for the keyhole when her hand found another hand in the dark.

"What are you doing?" asked a voice.

"Ahhh!!" whispered Paulette, and felt the blood drain from her soul. "Do-Do-Dolores?" she asked.

"Who think you it was? Your great-great-grandmother?"

"No, I—"

"I knock-knocked to see if you needed water. When you answered not, I assumed sleep had already found you."

"Oh... forgive me, Dolores, please, I was frightened."

Dolores spoke in the third person. "Old Dolores thought a tough Parisienne would have better things to do than believe such nonsense. But yet it's true: she did hang herself; with my child's eyes I saw her corpse. She had hung herself with old white rope, and easily you could see she was pregnant with her cadaver hanging. You know—her blue-white eyes—they never closed. They could never get them to close. Finally they had to sew them shut."

"Yes?"

"But it's a lot of nonsense, that walking around at night. Get some sleep and tomorrow I'll take you to the graveyard where your great-great-grandmother really is—when she's not in the house, that is. She must be quite rotten away by now, poor thing, smelly and fat worms slithering through her eyeball sockets. Well! I must to bed. Good night, Paulette."

Paulette bade good night quietly and returned to her room. When she was back in her bed she realized that she had not found out, as she wanted to, whether or not the key was still in the lock. She had seen an old trick in a play where, with an old-fashioned lock that you can look through, you push a piece of newspaper beneath the door until there's a lot of it just beneath the key, which protrudes like the head through the hole of a guillotine. You push a small object like a pencil through the lock until it pushes out the key, and then the key drops onto the newspaper, and you pull the newspaper toward you, gently, gently, and the key is in your hands and you can push it into the keyhole on *your* side of the door....

Paulette was lying wide awake, wondering whether a ghost in a room would have a newspaper and a pencil. No sooner did she have the idea than the entire proposition seemed rubbish: why wouldn't the ghost simply walk through the door, as ghosts normally do? Or for that matter, pass directly through the wall into her room? She turned away from the wall in the bed. She wondered: what would the ghost look like? Would it look the way it had when it died, or would it look as its former owner did now? If her great-great-grandmother was in an advanced state of decomposition, then the ghost would be little more than ectoplasm. Paulette thought this entire train of thought ridiculous. She then thought that ghosts, insofar as they existed, haunted specific places for specific reasons, and they were liberated from their torment by people praying for them, and she could not fathom why she should have anything to worry from *this* ghost. Unless, of course, she had done something she wasn't aware of, something that had nothing to do with assisting her father with theft. It was also possible, Paulette reasoned, that ghosts would visit the children of a sinner, in order to make them purge the crimes of their fathers.

Finally this proved too much. Paulette wanted to get up and see the room to remind herself, show herself, that it was empty. She got up; she could see quite easily by the moonlight; she walked through her door and ran her hand along the wall until she came to the molding, and then felt for the keyhole, when suddenly her hand vanished into a hole.

The door was open.

Aware it was open, unaware as to why it was open, Paulette started walking inside. She took a few tentative steps toward the back of the room, proceeding very quietly and sure that the exit was right behind her, when she was aware of a light filtering in. There was someone else in the room. Paulette stopped absolutely in midstep. But she was aware of this other body—quite definitely a body—in the room, suspended above her. As the light cleared and she became used to the darkness, she could see it: it was a decomposed, decaying body, shards of flesh hanging like strips of cloth from a corpse, the cloth itself musty, and in the head the skull peeking through and eyes open and white.

"Come," Paulette heard. "Come closer. Closer."

Paulette, who did not wish to show fear, stepped forward, and she was aware of the body extending two long hands toward her, reaching down, looking down from its hook, swaying a little softly. The hands clasped around Paulette's neck and began choking her; the grip was impossibly strong, impossible to break; she could feel the bone crushing, cutting....

She was waking up! She was screaming! Her room was filled with screaming!

In her room, sleeping next to Dolores, Marie heard the cry pierce the night, and she smiled.

The Bastiens were subtle and brutal. When Emile was in medical school, struggling, bent on graduating first in his class as he had done twice before, Robert de Saint-Loup, a real hellion, took an instant dislike to him and, with no motive other than proving class superiority, stole, sabotaged, and finally incinerated Emile's satchel, consigning to the winds a week's work. The cruel and aristocratic offender was so secure in his connections that with an insolent smile he tacitly admitted to the crime; Emile could but boil in rage. At the school, being well-connected was far better than being brilliant. Nevertheless, Emile projected revenge: by speaking to a professor he learned Saint-Loup was engaged to a porcelain princess of Saint-Germain, but that paradoxically he would soon be attending the wedding of a girl unknown to those circles. "A girl unknown" was parlance for a mistress: a beautiful, well-paid slut.

Emile stole a camera from the cadaver-dissection room and descended upon the wedding where Saint-Loup was an inexplicable guest. Emile had photographic skill and captured each expression on Saint-Loup's face. Later, he developed the pictures in his own bedsit, plastering windows and lining doors with black crêpe paper to make a darkroom. The best prints went to Saint-Loup with a note:

I had the honor of attending the wedding of—
—and——, and was able to take these photographs. I am sure that while these will provide sweet remembrance of things past for you, your fiancée will find their sight torture. I hope you will persuade me to destroy the negatives by confessing to the prefect that you destroyed my satchel. I can

assure you, sir, if you do not apologize, even the medicine you despise will seem serious in comparison to your name.

Saint-Loup's reply was swift: in the school corridors, he and a couple of his pals beat up Emile. Saint-Loup didn't even ask for the negatives—he assumed Emile would have sense enough to let the matter drop. In reply, Emile sent the photographs to the fiancée's family with a short note: "Please write for details." But she didn't. Saint-Loup was suspended for misconduct and threatened, to Emile's face, to disfigure it. From then on Emile carried a revolver. But Saint-Loup was expelled, his marriage was cancelled, and Emile graduated first in his class.

So that when he came to the Demarcation Line, his rear tire bulging with enough undeclared gold to send him to the camps, he had already learned a thing or two about staring down bullies.

"Good evening," said the border guard, a sergeant this time.

"Good evening."

"Your papers, please." Emile gave them to him.

"Aha! My friend told me we expected you back around this time. Did everything go well?"

"Yes, very well."

"Hmmm," said the guard.

"Something wrong?"

91

"Your tire... it seems to be flat."

"Oh?"

"Yes, I think you'd better come take a look at it."

Emile got out of the car, closed the door, strolled over to where the sergeant was shining a flashlight onto the tire. There were several privates, all with flashlights and guns, shining lights here and there.

Emile kicked the tire. "I'll be damned," he said.

"Do you want to change it here?" asked the sergeant. "Otherwise, the next service station is quite a ways up the road, and they'll be closed at this hour."

"No, no—you see—that *is* the spare. I haven't got another tire."

"Oh-oh—you're in a fix, then. Did you go over the pass near Montorgeuil?"

"Uhhh... yes."

"Lots of shrapnel on that pass. Probably burst one on the way, the other coming back."

"Well, I'll continue."

"Of course, if you had a *Volkswagen* tire..." said the sergeant, smiling.

"What can I say, Sergeant? I like French cars."

"Oh, a *patriot*!" said the sergeant. Since there were no cars behind him, there seemed to be no excuse not to have some pleasant, idle chat, while Emile's heart kept popping into his mouth.

The sergeant fidgeted, and his lips nibbled nervously. "I have to talk to you to make it seem

92

I'm interrogating you." He looked around cautiously. "I'm scared of going back to the front. I went, I came out alive. But now I'm even more scared to death of dying. Do you think the war will go on much longer?"

Emile was flabbergasted. Finally he said, "As long as everyone wants to fight.... If the last war was any sign, we have a long way to go."

"My papa died in the last one."

"My brother died in the last one."

"Well, that's just it, ain't it. Say, Doc. I have a hell of a stomach ache. All the time, now. Our doctor says there's nothing wrong with me. But—d'you think you could see me? I know you only see civilians...." The sergeant's face was outlined in the light. He was nineteen.

"No, I see soldiers too.... Priests. Everybody."

"Payment in kind? I'm not rich."

"Marks are better than francs."

"Yeah. Oh... one more thing." The sergeant looked around guiltily. "Have you got a cigarette?"

"No... sorry."

"S'all right, Doc. See you later?"

"Yes. Sergeant—thank you."

The sergeant straightened up and shouted some words in military French, and the barrier before the car lifted.

PART THREE

Back in 1944

CHAPTER FIVE

The war, now, was going badly. Major Schrödinger had always liked imagining his own death, watching himself with a smile torn apart at the hands of Resistants as if by harpies, or shot coolly and instantly by a sniper perched on an office building. He thought continually of his own death, and thought this state to be the natural state of a knight with a conviction of the cause. But now people in the street looked at him with undisguised hatred; youths stared with hatred and he wondered whether they were not hiding guns and practicing their aims, imagining a crosshair centered on his face.

When Major Schrödinger realized he no longer cared what his wife might suffer in Hamburg, once the Reich fell, he realized he had become jaded to the point of desiring self-destruction. He no longer had anything to live for, the war being lost and all his shared dreams of the Reich shot. Previously he had looked upon the peasants of Paris as a disorderly mob, helplessly self-divided, and which he would settle: he enjoyed the role of civilizer: the distance—the superiority—the worship. Guns, torture, intimidation, propaganda, organized terror—he did not call by those names these temporary wartime measures; it was discipline, order, safety, arresting murderers, executing poor losers, exterminating the enemy.

He was broken, after breaking so many people. He'd wanted the cold respect of every man; now, with all SS life so near its end, he wished to be touched. He had begun taking the bus just to feel bodies mashed against his; but men and women would retract from his uniform like snails from salt. He took to walking the streets in civilian clothes; more people bumped him accidentally, but he was surprised by how suspiciously they eyed him; every pupil searched for Gestapo. Surely we haven't done such a job on these poor people, he thought, but when he smiled experimentally people turned their heads as if he held a knife between his teeth.

There was the intense, horrible work at the prison: today, the prisoners come, go, are executed, are released; an endless succession of innocent, guilty, defiant, suffering faces; when he is supposed to sleep, he tosses from side to side as if at sea. Today, and tomorrow. Being an SS was supposed to have been like being a knight. Instead he found himself a hangman.

Schrödinger was sure his wife was waiting for him, and that made her more repugnant. He did not wish to wait. What meaning did their marriage have, now that the Reich was dysfunctional? He could smell defeat crouching in the air. He asked himself whether he had ever loved her. *No.* Absence had not made her dear: it made her dispensable. Amid the bustle of Paris he forgot her perfume and remembered her refusals. And then there was that icy period before the war—before their son had married; before....

Why? How? How could he send his own son *to his death*? He could've burst into the marriage ceremony, arrested everyone in sight. And spared his son; who was not Jewish, not really, not yet. But Rolf had said over and over and over: I love her, I love her, I love her. In the son was that passion the father had always at such expense destroyed in himself—but to his and his country's advantage, he thought; and he would teach Rolf a lesson, with his Jewish wife.

And then he had quietly asked to be posted in Paris, a city he'd always loved. Hitler was right: Paris taught lessons to Berlin. Schrödinger was not unpatriotic; he loved his country. But in Paris he could be a master among a conquered people and behind a proud mask of masterful cruelty admire, appraise, be amused, fall in love. He did not know how fragile was his mask until the first girl was tied to the torturer's stake: suddenly he became aware that women were courageous, often more courageous than the men. He could not send a woman to torture—not without trying to reason with her, plead, beg. No doubt Himmler and others would accuse him of weakness and excess of compassion: too dribbly a heart, and a mind insecure in its cold throne. But Himmler and others had lost the war.

Lost the war. War lost; lost war. The words played over and over in all their combinations and languages, like an anagram, all variations telling defeat. At the club several officers pooh-poohed the Americans, others pooh-poohed Stalingrad, others pooh-poohed the atmosphere of failure that was beginning to stink the club. Like so many he sensed disaster, but was not so desperate as to deny it while drinking. It was shame; shame to know that the people he'd so patronized and laughed at, that had caused him so coldly to assign gallows or firing squads for their failures, now thrust in his mouth the sour, iron taste of failure. And he was unhappy: he was alone. Another failure.

So long he had wished to spare Agathe at home the shame of knowing he was an adulterer. For her sake he'd called himself Christian; adultery was inexcusable. Loyalty to the state, to high ideals, was his mission and his pride. But every month he'd have a whore. At first he was patriotic even in bed: only German girls. But the years ground on, and German youth was ground up in the butcher shop of Stalingrad, and America began arriving with underwear and gunpowder and chocolate. Schrödinger knew Americans were fresh and that after ten years of struggle the Reich was stale. The Reich would starve, while America had a pantry miles wide, and bombers that could melt cities. Curiosity, then perversity—to control and enter flesh instead of land—drove him, like a bull being goaded by a picador, to a Frenchwoman. Yes, as a Christian, he'd been abominable: adultery, missing masses to shoot Jews. Another failure.

He wanted to blame the Jews for all his failures. But he was too noble, he thought. He'd seen Jews in various stages of death and they didn't seem scary. They seemed stepped on. In the early Reich, during the first days, despite the riots and the unpleasantness, so much seemed right and reasonable. But now— senseless, barbarous, brutish, nasty. He saw Jewish children slain—

And now, with his life crumbling around him, with him still inside it, like Samson's temple crashing down upon his own shoulders, with everything he'd worked for poised on the brink of collapse, he wanted of all things, understanding—touch—adoration—love. He wanted to adore another. In the way of his son.

Major Schrödinger had gone to museums and been startled by the way flesh—the pale, luxuriant, pink, white, or dark-chocolate-brown flesh—had been captured in the paint. He would feast his eyes on it, feasting on it as he had never done in Germany; drinking every wrinkle, letting his eye wander like a finger between the thighs, on the back, down the buttocks, down to where the hair began again; to that other pair of lips....

In imagination he grazed her skin, sent an exploratory patrol up and down her shoulders; scouting, looking for landmarks, crossing bridges of flesh; seizing territory: general of all flesh....

Boys had girlfriends; husbands, wives; but adulterous husbands had mistresses, and that made all the difference in the world. Girlfriends and wives were innocent; a mistress was illicit, guilty, shameful, pagan, delicious, sacred. No more whores, he told himself. One last love before the end. He knew there was but a limited time before he could no longer enjoy his mistress, any mistress. His sense of doom gave his wooing a courage he had never known in his life.

His *hôtel particulier* held a bed—large, noble; both its former owners were cinders floating over Poland. All over the house gold had been ripped from the boiseries, gold ornaments had been snapped off the staircase; gold had been wrenched out of the channels in the commodes and tables. All the ripped-off gold gave the place a plundered decadence, and flattered Schrödinger's new, cynical disaffection. He wandered around the house looking at the smashed glass, the broken windows, the cracked marble. *Sic transit gloria mundi.* Had they kept a dog? So many dogs in Paris had been eaten.

When he woke up with the first lancelike pain in his stomach, he knew his time in the Reich was nearly up. He had waited a few days to make sure the pain was real, and to punish himself. The penance having become too severe, he had gone, in excruciating pain and yet romantic, to Dr. Bastien's office.

And so he had met Simone.

At the second visit, the doorbell didn't work, or the elevator. So the major climbed the staircase, counting every step. There was something like a knife in his stomach, attached to his ribs; every step was like jabbing himself anew. He was sweating from pain when he entered the office.

"Doctor Bastien?" he called out. "Doctor Bastien?"

"Major!" said Emile. "Did you climb the stairs? You're quite mad. The electricity's out; it's quite impossible to operate."

"I am in a great deal of pain, Doctor."

"So is all of Paris—I don't mean to be flippant, but I can do nothing safely."

"What can you do unsafely?"

Emile stared at the major. "Perhaps... simulate conditions of a field hospital. Of the *First World War*. Simone?"

She entered the room, wearing a dress made of cotton, nurse-white but more daring, as if she were presuming spring was returning.

"Major Schrödinger wants to be operated on without electricity," Emile told her.

"He must have what he wants," she replied.

Emile waved and shook his hands, clouds of negatives. "No, I won't. You can't be in that much pain if you climbed the staircase."

"I can voluntarily withhold pain. You can operate on me without anesthesia."

Simone seemed amused. "You would collapse." The word "collapse" hung in the air. In the half-darkness of the office it referred to the end of the Reich.

"I am sick," the Major said. "I may die. I don't suppose your price has stayed the same?"

"It is risky for me, Major, to treat you, to

admit you into my office. My neighbors whisper. My children conspire...." He began talking when Heinrich Schrödinger and Simone Givry looked into each other's eyes.

You poor fool, she seemed to say, why don't you get out of France now?

Why don't you come with me? was his answer.

Emile kept talking—lights, pumps, sterility conditions, ether, increased risks, medical malpractice, and, finally, gold. "And so, Herr Major, my price has gone up."

"How much now?" absently asked Heinrich.

Emile seemed to hesitate. The three seemed like statues caught in a bronze light. "Double."

The major looked up as if he'd been slapped. "Double! Can you find a more tactful way to suggest the Reich is a rout? Doctor, you—why do you charge an impossibility?"

"Mein Herr, you are asking for an impossibility. A French doctor, operating without electricity to remove an ulcer from within an SS major's stomach, Americans at the gate of—"

"The Americans, nothing!" Heinrich shouted, slapping his hand hard on the table, and wincing in pain as his ulcer punished and stabbed him again.

"Major, you are in a great deal of pain," said Emile, restating the obvious and improving his bargain. "And if Americans are nothing, then who dug the crater in the Sacré-Coeur last night? Things are slipping. Marshal Pétain is here to inspect the damage—Americans to the west, Bolsheviks to the east, English

above, Resistance below, Jews everywhere—
no, Major, my price has gone up. It is dangerous
to be seen with a major; to give him medicine
for next to nothing is suicidal."

"Forty grams—is not 'next to nothing.' "

Simone's eyes concentrated upon herself,
upon a memory. She glanced at Emile, then
spoke to Heinrich: "Just last week, Major, a
friend of mine was arrested. The Gestapo is
still operating; terror is still angry and everywhere. She has disappeared."

"Who?" Emile asked Simone.

"Sylvie," Simone replied.

"I should have you both... arrested," said
the major, grunting, doubling over. "Not
doing so... that would be my... bargain."

"What would be the charge?"

"Failure... to comply with... failure... to col-
laborate..." The major was wheezing with
pain. Simone stepped next to him and touched
him. The major seized her hand; she let out
a cry of fright. "Please," he hissed. "Help
me." His gaze was longing, open, suffering.
Emile snapped his hands out of his white
pockets, and they froze in the air, ready,
deadly.

"I have nothing to live for. Take it out."

"Take what out?" asked Emile, brows furiously knotted.

Heinrich grabbed Simone's hand and covered it with overpowering kisses, closing his
eyes. "I have nothing," he said. "I am nothing.
Please, please, take it out, remove it, get rid
of me."

Emile put his hand on both of theirs. The major stopped kissing; pain began entering his face again. Gently, as if he were moving a hand through a wasp's nest, or lifting a bomb, Emile separated the two. Simone looked at him desperately and Emile nodded: Yes, I understand, he seized your hand without consent, no?

Still holding the major's hand, he lowered it, like a boom, to his side, without a word; there was only the *shhh* of the wool rubbing and the three breathing.

"She is not bargainable," Emile said.

"I am not bargaining. I am taking, offering. But I do not consider her any ordinary human being, as you do." He closed his eyes. "I cannot meet double."

"One and one half," said Emile.

"But... Doctor..." Heinrich smiled. "I want to die, you understand that."

"With that I cannot help you."

"Yes you will. You've done it before. I am asking for it."

"Major, I—no. I killed young men in France. I will never do it again."

"Yes, you will. Since I cannot have the girl."

"I said—she is *not bargainable!*" cried Emile, horrified, assaulted. But the German's gaze had such scary force that he backed into a corner of the office.

"Oh, 'one and one half,' " repeated the major, almost laughing, giddy. "And then, you kill me, yes? Only let me have the girl, my final conquest, my memorial of love. I am insane, my life is rage, my son's dead, my country shattered, my wife cares nothing; nothing and no one. That's all, that's everything. That's me."

The major sat up and, as if injected with adrenaline, began tearing off his jacket and vest. "One and one half," he repeated. "That makes—what?—sixty grams? Pretty good hangman's wages. I'll have the girl here, in this office."

"No!" screamed Simone. "No, no, I won't!" She raised her arms in a gesture of defiance and self-protection.

"Fight me! It will infatuate me. I have never wanted a woman that wanted me. I have never admired prisoners or human beings that cooperate. Conquest is joy. That is what it means to be a Nazi." He'd stripped to his chest. "Yes, Herr Doctor, sex, then operation. Maybe on the same table? I will be very relaxed." He jumped upon the examination table, every trace of his ulcer gone, his pain gone, manic excitement in his face. "One last conquest for Germany. Before the great retreat." He tapped the tabletop as if to show where a dog should leap, looking at Simone. And extended his hand toward her.

Emile had backed into a corner, his white smock sleeves protecting his face, his eyes, and his glasses. Simone was still standing in the middle of the room, her arms crisply folded before her breasts. Her hands were clenched tight, her wrists inwardly folded as if to protect them from the weeks of Allied bombing.

The German did not move—his hand remained before him, fingers outreaching selflessly, a gesture of friendship, of offered love. Emile and Simone had their hands wrapped tightly into themselves, cringing. Nothing moved. Then, slowly, the major's fingers closed like soldiers in a phalanx; the wrist rotated like a machine. He saluted. The exhausted hand and arm dropped to his side. Emile and Simone gradually regained their composure, realizing the German's insanity had subsided, like the bombing.

"Maybe you don't like my sense of humor," he said. "But I don't want to feel any pain anymore."

Finally Emile lowered his arms. "I can do that. For sixty grams."

"Payment after you operate. How else can I be sure I shall return living? Not for my family's sake—damn the Germans. But I have always wanted to see America."

"Sixty grams."

"I understand French, Doctor. One-and-one-half forty grams," he repeated in German.

"Simone," said Emile quietly. "I am going to wash. Prep the major."

★   ★   ★

Simone moved the razor with military precision across Heinrich's solar plexus, neatly cutting off each strand of hair. He was lying down.

"Can I breathe?" he asked her.

"Not too much."

She shaved each hair. Her delicate fingers felt the major's abdomen and tried to touch him without tenderness. He looked down at her, watching his underbelly, his navel ready. She smeared a brownish fluid over a square fifteen centimeters on each side.

"Will the cut be so long?"

"No—Emile says I don't know where he must cut, so I have to disinfect the whole area."

"Mademoiselle, I wonder if you love Herr Doctor."

"Altogether, Herr Major, I am not certain that I do."

"So why, may I ask, do you stay?"

"Hold still, or I might cut you—I missed some hairs here."

"Can I ask why?"

She met his eyes with two imploring disks, and then returned them to his stomach. "Herr Major. Sometimes, you've been doing something for so long you can't imagine not doing it. Custom stamps its die on even the most extraordinary love affairs."

Emile strode into the surgery with a mask over his face. "So! What has happened to all those Reich doctors I've heard so much about?" he asked.

"Well, Doctor," said Heinrich, still watching Simone smear more goo over his baby-naked belly, "the good ones work for Hitler. The medium ones are at the front. The bad ones are dead. Why do you wear a mask?"

"An American custom," answered Emile. "To keep my germs from entering your body."

109

"American?"

"Lie down." The major's toes were cold and bloodless.

"Are you comfortable?" asked the doctor.

"I feel like a cadaver."

"In a minute you won't even feel."

All the while Simone had been observing Heinrich—bald, with hair like strips of cloth hanging over his head. Uniformless, he looked pitiful, with nothing but what looked like a pajama opened at the stomach.

"Simone, light some more candles…. Adjust that mirror so that we get more light." Whispering: "Simone! Put the scalpels behind him, so he can't see!"

"I am not afraid of death," said the major, nonetheless turning his eyes away from the collection of razors and needles.

"It's never death, but the journey to death, that is fearsome. And the pain inflicted by the final door. I am going to etherize you. Or would you prefer I give you brandy? A bullet in your mouth? Suddenly I am back at Verdun, playing God, and without electricity. These, Major Schrödinger, are our candles—no electricity required. And this, Major, is the canister of Morpheus. It's kept under pressure—no electricity required. The hose attaches to this mask, which goes over your face." Emile suited the action to the word.

"Wait—may I speak—to Simone?"

Emile held the mask inches from Heinrich's face, pouring out twin nozzles of narcotics and oxygen, life and death, labeled blue and red. "If you insist." He turned away and with drama called: "Nurse! The patient wants to speak to you."

"In private," Heinrich added.

"Oh... ?" Emile raised his voice with sarcasm, then oozed out his doctor's smile. "Remember, Major. She's mine."

The major smiled thinly. "It's just that I want to go to sleep looking at a smile sincerer than yours."

The wrinkles beneath Emile's mask that indicated his smile fell. "Simone, come here. Put some more antiseptic on his belly."

"We've almost run out, Doctor. I am saving one last stash for use after the incision is stitched."

"Ah—yes. Sorry, Major, you're not supposed to know."

" 'Field conditions,' " Heinrich joked.

"Verdun. Well, Simone? Go on, talk to him. He wants to talk to you; for sixty grams, I won't interfere. Besides, the gas mixture needs correction, and only I can do that—ha!"

This time Heinrich looked at Simone, asking permission to take her hand in his. Frowning, lugubrious, she let him take it. Behind him the gas hissed.

Heinrich whispered. "Your hand—my God! Just holding it gives reinforcement."

"Major, if you don't mind my saying so, I'm not surprised you need succor. After killing—"

"Indirectly, Simone. Please." His eyes flashed with a sharp, brilliant idea. "So has your lover."

111

Simone raised an eyebrow and smirked. "No, Major, you won't convince me. It was his duty. They asked him to."

"It was mine too. They asked me," he answered fiercely. Simone looked away. But her hand remained caught inside his. Emile was not looking and pretended not to listen.

"Simone," Heinrich whispered, "after this, I am deserting. I am going to the Americas. We will be hated, unspeakable. But I have saved money!"

"My poor Heinrich, America will not want you, either."

"But *South* America! The same thing, only better food, and more dancing." He lowered his voice to a barely audible whisper. "I want you—to come with me. To the end of the world. No office, no doctors, no duties. There would be servants, horses, parties. You would be free. And you would be with me, in love with you."

"I am not a pawn. This is not a game."

"I am not bargaining. This is not a game. This is real. I am offering love."

"You know nothing about love," she said, tugging on her hand. But he held her tight. "I do."

The mask, plastic, transparent, with twin tubes that went to two tanks in red, blue, was suddenly near his face. Masked Emile held it in a gloved hand. "Simone, go change. The mixture is perfect and cannot wait."

But he still held her hand, and his eyes looked at her, smiling fondly. Simone stiffened her lips and arm and wrenched her hand out while Emile advanced with the mask. Heinrich chuckled, an echoed and muffled, hollow-sounding laugh inside his mask. "She loves you, Doctor!" he laughed. "Not me! Ha! Ha! Such luck! Is it the gas that makes me so airheaded?"

"Too much oxygen," said Emile solemnly, his rubber-protected fingers twisting a knob. But he caught Simone looking back at the major; he had flicked his eyes at the ceiling. He was looking at the black trails of smoke the burning candles had deposited. Emile scowled and gave Heinrich more narcotic.

In the office itself, Simone changed quickly, using the speed of slipping clothes on to take her mind away from impossibilities: the utter defeat of Germany, the possibility of slithering away to—what? another life? Was her life so bad? Was Emile so bad? What could she do, so far from Europe? She glanced at herself in the mirror and looked at Emile's massive, sculptured oak table. There were three photographs floating on the red leather sea: Marie, René, and Paulette. None of her. Looking into the mirror again, she pulled the mask over her face and entered the surgery.

She could tell from the crinkles around Emile's eyes he was neither smiling nor scowling, but wearing an expression of concentration so mute it was like a mask beneath a mask. "She is here," he said. "Now I'll let all the gas go. How do you feel now?"

"Sleepy. Pleasant. I am thinking... of..." His eyes fluttered around the room, halted on

Simone, then looked away, flickering like a dying light. He dropped into a narcotic sleep, a half-death with no dreams.

Emile sat down and looked at the major. Surely there could be no more vulnerable moment in a man's life than now. He could cut off his fingers one by one and the major would not move. He could kill him and his brain would hardly notice for at least five minutes.

His imagination ran riot:

"The major died on the operating table," he heard himself saying to Simone, meaning: Your Nazi suitor is dead.

"Oh, Emile, how could you??" she would scream, pounding her fists against him.

"An accident," he would reply, enjoying her tears. Yes, she had loved the German after all.

Or:

He was sitting on a creaky wooden chair, facing a tribunal, all shaven, wearing heavy eye-glasses, sour and serious. The date on the calendar hanging beside them, with a portrait of Hitler saluting, read 1946.

"So," said the man with the swastika round his arm, "in 1944 you thought we'd *lose* the war—because Anglo-Saxons bombed the Sacré-Coeur? Ha! Excusable, barely, but foolish, pitiful, pathetic! Yet, you idiotic quack, supreme mistake, you underestimated not only Luftwaffe power, and Wehrmacht power, but also the ingenuity of Gestapo coroners! They recognized your chloroform overdose. It's not malpractice. It's murder! An

SS, murdered! Emile Bastien, I sentence you—to be shot!"

Or:

The panel was Frenchmen wearing Gaullist crosses. The year was 1946, and a decorated Frenchman in regalia presided. "Chevalier Docteur Bastien, we congratulate you for disposing so neatly of one of Paris's most notorious criminals." Every member of the board, now all bearded, patrician, kindly, and with rosettes in their lapels, pumped his hand. He imagined the Légion d'Honneur being hung round his neck, the citation reading: "For his services to France during the wars, 1914–1918, 1939–1944." At medical schools where he would teach the students would whisper, "He killed an SS under anesthetic. Wow!"

Emile was back in the operating room, watching the major breathe the forced-sleep gas, watching the chest rise and fall. Coming out of his reverie, he said, "I'll sew up the ulcer first. It will seem less suspicious." Automatically, Simone nodded. Automatically Emile got the sterilization fluids uncorked and dipped his sponges. Automatically he smeared the brownish fluid over the shaved area of the stomach.

"Did you water this down?" he asked.

"I had no choice," Simone replied, muffled by her mask.

He chose a number-five scalpel—medium length. He had heard that some doctors did nothing except look at the ulcer and tell assistants where to cut, where to sew; he, Emile, would do it all himself.

"Simone, you are aware of who—of what—this consciousness—this lack of conscience—is." He meant the major.

"I know."

"Good," said Emile, and made the first cut.

It was a nice, elegant cut, neatly exposing the stomach under the lungs. So, thought Emile, here we have the Nazi physiology. There doesn't seem to be any difference, although Emile half expected to find swastikas tattooed on the inside. Emile had hoped to find the ulcer on the superior part of the stomach; no luck. It was there, underneath.

With a gloved hand, he pushed the stomach, and it deflated easily. From the looks of it, it was completely empty: the major had more than followed his instructions; he had exceeded them—his entire digestive system looked empty. He clearly meant to survive this operation.

Emile poked around some more, looking up occasionally at the anesthesia machine, which kept pumping away happily. Under his plastic mask the major looked placid, even content. Go on, he seemed to be saying; I've a normal body, a normal brain, normal stomach.

Emile could see the diaphragm, opening and closing like a squeeze box, and he prodded the stomach, lifted it, placing metal clasps to hold it up, out of the way. Emile crouched down, tried to look deeper into the patient, caught a glimpse of the dark liver, brown, enormous, looking relatively unused. By raising himself up far over his patient, Emile could see the tangled white folds of the upper intestine, like a giant white worm coiled in the man's gut; no, there was nothing particularly exciting about a Nazi inside. Any differences would probably be between the ears, but he didn't have a saw and wouldn't have known what to look for anyway. Perhaps their brains were flattened at their rallies. Underneath was the knowledge that there was no difference, physically, between an SS and an FFI. Just a change of armband.

He lifted the stomach. There, in the most awkward place imaginable, was the ulcer, and it was enormous. The poor major must have been writhing with pain. Had he been delirious? Emile imagined he saw the hydrochloric-acid digesting fluid spilling out of the stomach and into the thoracic cavity; but that was his imagination, he thought. With infinite care not to pierce the delicate liver, he raised the stomach, attaching it to the sternum, until it was almost out of the body. The anesthesia was very smooth, and he had hours left to commit murder.

He selected a number-one needle, the grossest, to start, and he took out a patch from Simone's waiting fingers and cut it to size. Then, like a seamstress, he threaded the needle, and—this was his favorite part—he started sewing up the stomach, using a mirror placed underneath to watch what he was doing. He hated the mirror; everything felt wrong, backwards; but it was such a large hole, and this body looked so healthy, he could go quickly and grossly around the wound.

"Simone," he said. She grunted to acknowledge. "I'm hungry. In the kitchen—there's some Roquefort. Bring it, and a knife. Get a knife from the kitchen sink, if you can."

"You want to eat? Now?"

Emile had turned with his furious concentration back on the sewing. Too spooked to understand, she left the room.

The operation was simple, and Emile was nearly done. He lowered the stomach into place, patted it as if to reassure it that everything was all right, that it would get lots of bratwurst in the future, and squished and squeezed the organs back into place. Simone appeared at the door, like a surreal waitress in a surgeon's mask.

"Good. Bring it here. Set it next to the scalpels." Simone, her eyes as wide as mirrors, set down the plate. Calmly—disconcertingly calmly—Emile took the knife plucked from the standing water of the kitchen sink and drove it deep into the Roquefort, twirling it around the blue and moldy cheese.

"Vive la France," he whispered.

Inside the major there was a flap of skin pitched open like a tent. The seam beneath made a smooth surface, not unlike a rubbery pastry. Emile honed in the knife and like a

118

gourmet wiped it on the inside of his incision, dumping all the cheese inside the body, right next to the ulcer.

"It would be a neat trick, to get out of this," Emile said. He replaced the blunt knife back on the cheese plate and gave it to Simone. "Delicious," he said, "but I'm not as hungry as you thought. Take it back. Wash it very well." And he turned away.

"Emile... ?" she asked.

"What wonderful skin he has! They feed the SS well even now. No ersatz butter. No wonder butter costs eight hundred francs; he gets it all, lucky devil. Shall I use a fine needle? It will take twice as long, and use up the rest of my anesthetic. But don't we want the work to look professional? We want to make sure Hans is getting his money's worth. Silk thread? Yes, I think that'd be best. Only high-class stuff. Only the best Roquefort, ha, ha!"

"Emile?" repeated Simone.

"Yes, Simone. Go wash the plate."

"Have you killed him?"

Emile let out a furious, controlled sigh. "Are you defending your lover's life?"

"Lover? I never touched him!"

"Exactly. When I say 'lover,' of whom do you think? You *should* think me. He'll soon be dead; the time it takes bacilli to proliferate to ten or two hundred million. Slow agony; delirium before brain failure. Justice? So much for my Hippocratic oath; I broke that long ago. Along with my marriage oath. Any other oaths I do not know. How talkative I am, and slow you are. Why is that plate not washed?"

"Emile, you haven't..."

"No, *you* haven't—and absolutely not, *I* haven't, you stupid idiot. If you want to turn me in, go on, say I have. Will that help you? Or hurt you?"

"Emile—you've descended to his level, killing—"

"I'm beginning to think you knew him better than you've told me. Should we prolong this, or cut the anesthesia? Maybe he'll want to join this conversation. Go put that plate back, washerwoman, and let the doctor finish."

"Emile, you *smartass*! If he dies, the SS will seek you—"

"And find a doctor who has treated more Germans than Frenchmen, whose medical record is blameless, who has never made a medical error in his life. Only *you* can hurt me now. Hurry, wash, go; I must sew!"

Simone, aghast, left with the plate, crashing into the door. René was standing on the other side.

"That brat again," Emile said, concentrating like a sorcerer, necklaces of sweat forming on his forehead, watching the meter in the anesthesia bottle go downward and downward. "Only the best doctor! And the best Roquefort!" he whispered, and chuckling like a Norse Fate, selected a fine needle, good for petit-point, and a spool of beautiful silk thread. What a waste of an immaculate suture.

120

Like Atropos, who ended men's lives, he cut the thread.

"Simone?" asked René, beyond the door. "Is Daddy operating?"

"Yes, he's operating. He's operating on an SS major."

"Is he eating, too?"

"No; this was for the patient."

CHAPTER SIX

The *hôtel particulier* had two stories and was set in a cobblestoned courtyard in the rue de Grenelle. A bum was living where the stable once was; he scurried away when he heard footsteps approach. In the afternoon the place didn't receive much light, and the skies were swirling with clouds, so the two shadows were diffuse, a woman's and a man's. A strong hand took the knocker and beat it upon the door.

"There's no answer. This is a stupid idea, Simone. Let's go back."

"He *said* he would be here, though. Try again, please, Father."

Father Nicolas again rapped upon the door. "He's certainly not here. It's a joke, a lie. Maybe a trap? Who knows what the Resistance will do. Come, Simone, let's leave; I don't want to cause any trouble."

"Father—*I* want to see him, I don't care what you or Emile say, and I won't be stopped now. Please—knock one more time."

A crowd of boys, famished and dirty, making their way from the streets where they'd been rummaging through garbage cans, started approaching them.

"Simone, we're not safe. Let's leave."

"I'm sure he's here, Father, please. He promised me."

"What does it mean, a promise from a Nazi, now?" The priest looked at the urchins, getting closer, and hissed. "Scat!" he said. The boys did nothing more than flinch and pause in their slow advance.

"Simone, please. These boys are going to shake us down."

"Boys!" she said, and smiled. "Boys! Listen to me." They paused again, pricking their ears at the voice like a bell. "Do you know if someone is inside this building?"

"Yah," one of them said. "Major Schrödinger."

"Do you know if he's still inside?"

"We're hungry, mam'selle."

"I can get you food."

"Get it. We'll tell."

"But is he inside?"

"Obviously, Simone, he's not! These boys are just trying to trick you! Shame on you boys! Go away!"

The boys began approaching, hissing like little serpents. They rattled their tongues inside their mouths and, hunching forward, with dirty sandals, stained clothing, discolored skin, and their eyes big and ringed with black like raccoons', they hissed.

"Get away! Leave!" Father Nicolas moved his arms around, and his sleeves swished before his face; the crucifix swayed as if upon a swing.

"*Les enfants! Les enfants!*" Simone cried.

"Git us food, and we'll git you in!" cried the eldest boy, the strongest. He was wearing a swastika and an FFI armband, one on each arm.

"You *must* have some food!" Simone said to the priest.

"Of course not! Help! We're being mugged!"

And indeed one of the boys was already pawing at Simone, and she felt little hands, black hands, tiny fingers, gripping at her purse; she realized they were a girl's hands, not a boy's.

"Oh, God!" she cried. "Leave it!"

"Give it! Give it!" they cried in their tiny, raspy voices.

"ALL RIGHT!" cried Simone, with a god-like force that surprised them all, most of all herself. "I have connections! You touch this priest, you touch me, and you'll see! Pathetic children—you'll get what you're looking for! You want food? You'll get it. Food and money. But right now, back off, you—Nazis, or whatever the hell you are!"

The children didn't obey, but they stopped. Two of them had gripped hard Father Nicolas's soutane. They did not let go. And fingers still held Simone's leather.

"Rat, let go of my purse!"

"Not a rat!" shrieked a little voice; her fingers held fast.

"Let go!" Simone was shaking inside, horrified, but overlooking them all was a window; she was sure it was Heinrich's bedroom, or the room leading to it. He would hear them— someone had to!

Reluctantly, the fingers opened. Simone saw hands grasping the priest's robes, but she knew how to open those too. "Here," she said, snatching the precious object in her purse and holding it high. "Ration card!" Suddenly the hands, the arms, detached themselves from the silk of the soutane, and like arms at a rally, all upraised, reached for hers, held high. "Wait! This card's good... only if I sign it." Feeling like throwing up and yet miraculously strong, she said, "Open the door! Get us inside!"

The children froze. But the eldest boy, the one wearing the armbands, detached himself from the group and in two athletic strides stood on the doorstep. He and Simone exchanged glances; he looked at the light-blue ration card held high as the Grail. She nodded, indicating she would give it to him. Then he reached beneath the doormat and found a key fitting the lock. Simone and Father Nicolas watched wide-eyed, but the children didn't ever take their eyes off the card while the door opened soundlessly.

"The card! The card!" they all shrieked.

"Policeman!" yelled Nicolas. "Help! These children are assaulting us!"

A policeman was walking past the entrance to the courtyard, and he smiled beneficently when he saw the ragamuffins, in tatters, dirtily reaching toward Simone.

"That's good!" he called out, with a congratulatory, patrician tone. "Just don't overdo the charity, miss!"

"Piss off," whispered Simone beneath her breath, and signed the card. "Boy!" she yelled. The eldest, leaping and crawling over the ragged heap of other boys, was next to her. She held the card before his face. "Now get out of here."

"Who d'you think'll win?" he asked.

"People who keep their mouths shut," she replied, and gave him the card. Instantly, amid primate-like screeching and calling, the boys and girls were running and shrieking across the courtyard. Behind Simone and Father Nicolas the dark door beckoned like a grave. Someone was inside.

Simone bounded in and almost closed the door on Father Nicolas, who had been crossing and recrossing himself. "My case!" he cried. "They took my case!"

Simone was inside the dark salon; it smelt of decomposition; something was rotting; a pipe had burst and on the ceiling, amidst the magnificent, raped boiseries, a vaguely urinous yellow water stain was spreading like a halo.

"They took it!" he repeated, groping his soutane like a man desperately searching for his wallet, just pickpocketed. "The filthy bastards! The scum!" He ranted; Simone would not listen, and stumbled into the salon, where a grand piano kept watch like a sleeping lion.

It was missing its white keys like the teeth in the urchins' mouths; and some of the strings had been cut away, dangling crazily outside its box. Simone remembered hearing rumors Nazis strangled their prisoners with such wires; she bent over and was sick right on the ancient carpet.

"The criminals! They should be arrested! Put away!" raged Father Nicolas. "Filthy! Dirty! Simone—where are you?" he said, speaking to the shadow kneeling on the floor— all the shutters had been closed. "You hear me. I can't do it without the unguents in my case. It would have no value. Not to God. I have to go back. I'm sorry. It's just—this house, it's wrong somehow, Simone, I can't give it to a— well, look!" He was talking to himself, to a congregation hidden in shadows, not to her. "Sorry." And with that he opened the door, walked outside, and clacked it shut.

Simone was alone in the room, though not in the house. Still panting horribly, feeling out of control, dirty, sick, and invaded, she felt: It's not worth it. It was all a horrible, horrible mistake. Heinrich would have signaled his presence by now. Or was it a trap?

"Heinrich?" she called out into the gloom. "Heinrich?" At the entrance, a dark silhouette appeared. Simone started, stared, horrified; it was like seeing a ghost.

"Herr Schrödinger is upstairs. He is close. Where did the priest go?" It was an old woman's voice, a crone, with a nose hooked like a beak and the lips scowling downward.

She looked outside the window, through the shutter slats. "So. He found his case. The children took it not. Upstairs, Herr Schrödinger. Quick. He is close."

She indicated the stairway with a bony, knobbly finger; her sleeve widened and thickened; then she dropped her hand like a lightning bolt and disappeared through a doorway.

The staircase was circular. A metal rail ran along the side of it; where marqueterie had been inlaid with precious metal, only knife gougings remained. Simone gripped the banister, and in her ears voices whispered all this was folly, but step, by step, by step, she ascended. Every stair was cracked. The landing had a frame: in the bottom of it was a medallion marked FRANCISCO GOYA Y LUCIENTES. But the frame was empty.

The hallway had two doors. The first led to a room stripped of furniture. She walked to the dusty window and looked outside, across the courtyard. Still on the porch of the house was Father Nicolas. Strangely, he had his head down, and his hands clasped, as if he were praying, but facing away from the house. He clasped a rosary in his hand, and bowed, and bowed, as if counting off beats.

Simone wiped her mouth. Did this mean so much to her? There was one door, and after closing her eyes and asking God for help, she walked across the hall and opened it.

Between the posts of the fourposter bed hung a giant red-and-black swastika, large enough for a rally. On the mantelpiece was a hand-sized effigy of Hitler's head, but dam-aged; only half his head was present: only the stern eye, the waxed hair, told an identity. Various portraits, broken, their protective glass cracked, hung on the wall; and in the air, scattered over various parts of the room, were the uniforms of an SS major, black, silver, emblazoned with decorations for bravery, valor, every kind of courage, shining, myste-rious, and empty.

In the bed, gaunt, hideous, horrible, his teeth gritted, his white fists clutching sheets stained with blood, the major was hardly aware of Simone's entrance. The whole room, filled with his meaningless and about-to-fall-into-catastrophe memorabilia, was actually filled, as if with a watery element, with gasping. He who had sent so many to the wires of the piano was fighting for each breath in a twenty-four-hour agony that had lasted, thanks to Dr. Bastien's science, not twenty minutes, but seven days.

His face was somewhere between white and green. "Heinrich?" said Simone, watching him, not daring to get any closer, the lime stench as strong as a cordon of gas-masked policemen round his bed. "Heinrich?" she said again. He suddenly snapped open his eyes, as if hearing a human voice for the first time.

"Si-..." He couldn't finish her name. He gath-ered all his power for a single word, keeping at bay as if with an iron sword the fire in his stomach. "Come."

Faced with fear, Simone could not. "I came—"

Heinrich's face turned into mute anger, frustration at being unable to speak a single word, pain so intense he could hardly think. He opened his mouth, and breath passed his lips, soft as thunder, but his speech was strangled in his throat.

Simone said, "I brought... a priest. But... he won't."

"Never... panic," Heinrich said. "Stay... stoical," he said, swallowing. Then he coughed, "Ugh! Ugh!" Bile spilled from his white lips. "Do something," he said. "Anything."

Simone walked over to the window and threw it open. It led out to the back of the courtyard. She called: "Father Nicolas! He's here!"

"Ni-colas?" Heinrich said.

Simone paid no attention, but banged on the frame of the window, worn down with rain and the elements, until splinters came off easily in her hand. She turned round. "You goddamned fool, you certainly picked a fine place to die in."

"Decorations—splendid," he replied, and now his every breath was taken as if through a long, dry tube—breathing through a keyhole. Simone waited by the door; her legs would take her no closer to him.

Then, sweaty and winded, Father Nicolas stumbled in, wildly looking round the room. He asked, desperately but hopefully, "Am I too late?" He pointedly looked everywhere in the room, registering with waves of shock, as if he were being struck again and again across his face, with the deranged, lugubrious artifacts.

Simone pointed at the bed with a single telling finger.

"Mother of Jesus," Nicolas said. He crossed himself and kissed the crucifix that hung round his neck. "Is he dead?" he asked, his pudgy face flickering with the hope that duty might have flown away after all, with Heinrich's soul—perhaps down to hell?

"Go help him. I don't dare come near."

"You're the one who brought us here," the father said. He visibly gathered his courage, as if plucking a handful of thyme from a garden deep in his soul. Straightening up, he walked past her with false pride. Simone saw only his white collar shining. He suddenly blew up with professionalism. *"In nomine patris—"*

Heinrich was trying to sneer. "Hallo—Nic."

"—et filii et spiritu sancti." The priest outlined in the air above the bed a fiery, ethereal cross. The priest leaned over like a dentist, and his manner was a parody of kindness. "Good afternoon... Major. Hiya, Hen."

"No... salute?" chided the major, slipping into a toothy grin. "Too informal? American?"

The priest had his fingers curled lightly upon the bed. Now he lifted his pinkie in a miniature, Lilliputian Reich salute.

"Gut. Reich not dead yet," said the major, his eyes slipping sideways under their lids.

The priest's eyes, animated with interest at imminent catastrophe, flickered all over the room. "So, where do you keep the bodies? Have you kept any of the execution notices?"

130

Simone cringed. "Father—"

"I know what I'm doing," he said blandly. "Anything you want to confess? Murder?"

"Yes."

"Treason?"

"Never."

"Adultery?"

"Not really."

"Anything else?"

"Abandoned... wife."

"That's awful. Do you think you can say a few Hail Marys for me, son?"

"No... Father."

"I'll say them for you." The priest closed his eyes and said unintelligible syllables. To Simone it seemed the priest was not even pausing for commas or anything but rumbling on as fast as he could. "That's that. You're sure you haven't committed adultery?" Heinrich's head was turned on its tight neck, looking past the priest, looking at Simone. Nicolas thought it was fatigue, or some sort of paralysis that would take the sinner to hell frozen, but then he realized he was looking at her. He turned around. "Not even in your heart?"

Heinrich nodded softly, like a shamefaced boy. Or a bird, hoping to drink from the pool of mercy.

"Well, adultery in the heart is just as bad. Pity God punishes for wanting as for doing, but I don't make the rules. Another Hail Mary." Again he rattled off the prayer, not pronouncing anything, his lips vibrating like stitching machines; only faked fervor indicated it was even prayer.

Father Nicolas finished and opened his eyes, glanced over his shoulder, then looked back at the major. "But... let us admit. She is beautiful. Isn't she?"

The major nodded, weakly but happily. "But Nic. She's not married. Not adultery."

"Oh, that's right! I guess she's the one who... Let's just say the Hail Mary is for her account, not yours."

"Yes." They smiled together, the priest holding a tubby finger beneath his nose to conceal his smile, and the major erupting into a volcanic spate of coughing and horror. "But," he added, "me married. Me."

"Oh?" said Father Nicolas, his amusement fading. Simone, not understanding what they were laughing about, laughed too, and ran a hand through her shoulder-length hair. The priest looked at her crossly, then turned back to his charge. "Well... Major, the prayer may as well be for you." He smiled and tried to take the major's fist. But the fist was wrapped tight around the sheets, as if the major were holding on to it for life. The charcoal-red stain of blood was seeping through the sheets, all the way up to the blankets, and seemed closer.

Father Nicolas again reached deep for another handful of strength, and straightened his shoulders. "Now. Last one."

"Worst one."

"Murder? Many murders? Sin of violence—mortal?"

"Mortal. Yes. Terrible sin. Must confess."

"Whom have you killed, Major?"

The major stopped breathing. Throughout the room was a ghastly afternoon silence; another power outage, and the beginning of a retreat from Paris—horses, cars, Nazis, going, gone.

"My son," the major said. The hand twisted around the sheets, the knuckles looked ready to pop from beneath the skin. The major was shaken like a marionette by a convulsive fit, his body shaking like a child shaking a toy. "Forgive me!" he yelled, in a disastrous, dry-as-chalk voice. "Forgive me!" he tried to say, and began moaning, and whimpering like a dog about to be whipped, a cur.

Father Nicolas raised a fist closed tight to his mouth. The other clenched a rosary, which dangled and shook like a wind ornament caught in a storm. "Nothing..." he began. "Nothing... is worse.... Abraham... and Isaac..."

"Yes, but he didn't, I did!" the major cried.

"Dear God—I cannot—not my power.... Whom... whom else have you... killed, Major?"

"No one, no one else! My son, only my son!"

Simone found she'd collapsed into a chair, the only other chair, sitting on a pile of white shirts, the ones with the knifepoint collars. The conversation seemed to be happening very far away, as at the far end of a tunnel or the wrong end of a telescope. She had seen the bloodstain before; now it seemed to be

133

spreading across the carpet, up the walls; the whole room was painted in blood, blood for a sacrifice. She too held a fist to her lips.

Father Nicolas's hand was shaking as he drew a trembling cross in the air. "Major Heinrich Schrödinger, I will pray for your sin. 'The Lord is my shepherd, I shall not want. He—' "

"Not prayer. Forgiveness!" the major hoarsely tried to cry, his lungs damp, his throat parched, his eyes terrorized and wide as a lamb's on the altar. The hand that had been gripping the sheets pounced like a deadly insect upon the priest's sleeve; it fastened upon the meat beneath and pressed hard, with a strength born of desperate, craven fear. "I could've stopped him! But I didn't! I had my orders! Father, you can understand me, since we both gave our lives to a higher cause, our country, our god—I, I, I a knight!"

"Major—"

Simone stood up. She took several paces toward the major and took his hand in hers. "Let go," she said. "He can't—give you extreme unction... if you don't let him!"

"Extreme unction?" gasped the major. "Forgiveness?"

"Let go," she repeated. The major looked at her with the innocence of a child, wide eyes full of hope. "Father," she said, "you have your unguents? This woman downstairs— said you'd found your case."

The major's fingers released. He was looking at the priest, who had quick-glanced at Simone.

"Woman?" Nicolas repeated. "There's a woman downstairs?"

"My maid," said Heinrich. "Loremarie. She's attending me. I think she's insane, but she attends me."

Simone looked at the major and then at the priest. "Get this over with," she said quietly.

The major was mouthing forgiveness with dry lips.

Fingers on oils, crossing the forehead: from the arsenal of unguents the priest dispensed mercy, quickly. Visibly the major's breathing calmed like rain at the end of a storm; already he was staring at the swastika, his eyes fixed ahead as if on the stars.

"Amen," the priest said, and snapped the case shut. He crossed himself with the speed of a fencer tracing a cross with his foil. "It is accomplished," he said, with a trace of irony. He looked at the swastika hanging over the bed, then glanced at the major.

"Do you mind?" he said. He went over to the pins holding the swastika in place.

"Would better be... Mary Magdalene?" Heinrich said softly. He was lying very dignified on his back, his arms alongside his body.

The priest unpinned the flag from the bed. For a moment the flag hung defeated, impotent. But then Nicolas pinned it back up, using a single corner. It hung sideways, and the upset swastika was listing. From within its folds you could see only the black bars horizontally and vertically intersecting in a field the color of blood.

"Makes more of a cross, don't you think?" Nicolas asked.

"Christianity... and the Reich... very similar," said the major, smiling.

"So you approve?" said Nicolas, smiling tightly but sincerely.

Heinrich nodded peacefully.

Father Nicolas took a place by the foot of the bed, and with his fingers interlocking, the Bible clutched between them, rattled off lots of Latin like machine-gun fire. The ceremony was capped with an Amen that fell like a curtain.

"Amen," said Simone, and crossed herself. The major had already crossed himself, his hand moving slowly, creeping along, the hand of a man slowly drowning in his own body.

Instead of "Amen," Heinrich blurted out, "Infection... spreading."

"Cankers are for the physician of your body. But I am a physician of your soul." He whispered to Simone: "We've done *everything* possible for him. It's God's problem now."

"There must be something more we can do."

"Not our problem. Let's leave. Emile is waiting for you."

"I'm not going back, not with you, not yet. Let me talk to him."

"Simone—why? What can you possibly

accomplish? It is all accomplished," he said, with sarcasm, winking toward heaven. "And I don't want to have to meet those boys again."

"Well, deal with them yourself! You're a man!" And she ripped herself from his hand and strode over to the bed, sitting down next to the major. From her seat she looked at Nicolas and grimaced, like a cat baring fangs: Leave, she told him.

Father Nicolas, too scared and confused to say anything, nearly tripped on his soutane as he about-faced and headed out the door. His pudgy jowls appeared for a moment in the doorway; he was asking with his eyes if she wanted the door shut. She nodded furiously, so he shut the door with a quiet click.

Nicolas looked around the landing, for something to steal. Even if there was a woman in the house—the housekeeper—still, she would be downstairs. So much was gone, so much taken! These were Jews of good taste; someone had wrested a Mantegna from its frame. His covetous eyes ran along the empty places where statues once were—probably everything had been shipped to Berlin as booty. Surely the Nazis had forgotten something? He flung covetous eyes around and around....

Heinrich's room was hushed, quiet as a sepulcher. Heinrich counted his breaths as if they were each numbered, counting down toward the last.

"Heinrich..." Simone began.

137

He was still on his back, lying still, flat, dignified, his breathing focused, even tranquil. She repeated his name. The swastika stirred lazily; there was a breeze coming in the room from somewhere.

"Yes?" he said.

"Do you really think you're forgiven?"

"Yes," he replied with quiet, spiritual confidence. "What the priest does... is good enough for me." He was speaking infinitely quietly, almost without employing his vocal cords, or windpipe, but direct-carving the words on his breath; and Simone was so close she could see the sculpturing of his lips.

She looked down at herself. "Some say it is for man to judge, not God."

"They're wrong," he announced. "Besides... you're the one who brought him here. It's true, I asked you. Did Emile—"

"Emile was opposed."

"Simone—please. One last favor. My medals... there on the dresser."

On the dresser were disks of metal, vaguely discolored, with strips of faded color behind them. There were four, each one of them round, with assorted devices, plumes, indentations.

"Pin them," he said. "On my pajamas. I haven't got the force to, anymore. I want to die perfect. Pin my medals on for me."

Simone took a medal. She imagined it covered with blood.

"You're so beautiful," he continued. "This—

kaf! kaf! kaf!"—coughing—"this is what it must be like, to be swept away, dead from the battlefield, by a Valkyrie. You're my Valkyrie, Simone!"

Simone fingered the medal; it was cold and black. "What is this for?" she asked, quietly.

"That? Bravery under fire. I saved a man's life earlier in the war. A doctor; I carried him after he was hit."

"Why not an Iron Cross?"

"Not—brave—enough," he said, trembling. "Say nothing. Don't judge me."

The door to the bedroom creaked open. "Major?" It was Loremarie, the servant. Simone looked at her as if aggressively defending her right to be next to the major. "Major, the priest is trying to steal the salt cellars. He put them in his pocket. Should I—?"

"Kill him," Heinrich said. Then he laughed, and the laughter asphyxiated itself in a dry, noiseless cough. "No. Are the salt cellars yours, Loremarie?"

"They are ours," she replied. "Or no one's." She spoke in a thin voice, like underwater crackling.

"You know, Simone," the major said merrily, "I used to do that; I would say 'Kill him!' and they would. So much power, once...."

Simone looked at the strange crone in the door. "You don't add all those 'Kill thems' to your—?" She carved the word "murder" with her lips.

Heinrich shook his head. "They weren't...

139

human beings, those. Were they, Loremarie?"

"Not at all," she said, in that same fragrant, awful voice. "They were Jews."

"We gave them all a chance to leave."

"You did not."

The major was thinking Nazi thoughts. "I don't remember.... We must have? Did we not?"

"Should I let him have the salt cellars?" Loremarie said again, that sexless, droning voice.

"Yes! By all means. A salt cellar is a small price to pay for forgiveness. The silver ones?"

"*Ja.*"

"I won't need those anymore." He turned to Simone. "My life outside the Reich has been worthless, Simone. If you won't pin those medals on me, I'll have Loremarie—"

He erupted into coughing, awful coughing, and his hands gripped the side of the bed hard. The bloodstain on the sheet seemed to have crept up to his heart, and Simone saw fluid dripping from the lace, falling on the floor. It was a flood of bile and piss; the major was drowning in his own body, and coughing, gasping for air that would no longer enter his nauseated lungs. Then he died: in one shuddering spasm that wrenched open his jaws and contorted his face like a mask stretching to the breaking point. Inside his dark mouth, his blue tongue twisted and writhed like an obscene caterpillar, articulating nothing, and his entire body arched as if reanimated by electrical lightning. It froze in mid-convulsion: back arched like the bridge over the final river, face screaming nothing, eyes staring and empty. The medals had fallen onto the floor, covered with fluids from his stomach.

In the dripping aftermath of the lethal convulsion, Simone backed away as if from death itself. Heinrich was staring ahead at his flag. Her legs carried her backward, one hand extended before her as if for protection from his malignant presence, and she backed into the door, hiding her face with her hand, looking away. Outside, a bird twittered. Facing him, not daring to turn her back toward his cadaver, she fumbled behind her for the doorknob—it wouldn't turn, it was stuck. "Help!" she cried. "Help!" The doorknob twisted, the door opened, and Father Nicolas, carrying a painting under one arm, entered. She shot into the protection of his black folds so fast he felt assaulted and staggered backward, toward the landing of the staircase. One foot descended one step, he dropped the painting, but he held firm balance. Simone's mouth and eyes were a wordless, tearless weeping; she clutched the folds of his soutane while the painting slid step by step down the staircase. Loremarie, standing at the bottom of it, watched it fall.

"He is dead, is he not?" she asked quietly, addressing no one, but her voice walked up the steps.

The priest held Simone and looked over his shoulder to watch his painting bound down. It came to rest facedown halfway along the staircase. "Simone, we must leave," he said.

Without releasing her, or looking at what was beyond the door, he closed it. "Accomplished, then, in the nick of time," he said. "Come. Let's go."

"Nicolas... my purse... the major."

"Don't waste time! Go get it!" He opened the door, again without looking inside; in fact, he deliberately turned his face away. "Quickly!"

Simone stepped back into the sepulcher, and tried not to look at the out-of-focus, peripheral view she had of the major's rigor mortis spasm. Picking up her purse, she saw a hand, a mouth, a medal. She almost looked back, and was gone; the door clicked shut.

"Thank God for that," the priest said, and very solemnly traced some more crosses on the door. "He's lucky I don't make a swastika and give his spirit wrong directions," he said, bouncing down the steps, almost jolly. He picked up his painting and held it up, frame and all. "Poussin? I doubt it. Still, quite pretty."

Simone saw the priest holding a swirl of foggy, dark colors, but descended the staircase, running a gloved hand along a balustrade, step by step. Suddenly the house seemed painfully fragile—the chandelier like an army of crystals flying above the staircase. She took small steps. Loremarie had again vanished.

At the landing, the priest tried to take her hand, but she pulled it out from his grasp. "Please," she said. "I'm a married woman."

"Oh, are you?" said the priest, doubting with puckering lips. He trotted on into the courtyard, squinting his eyes like machine-gun slits, looking for renegade boys. "I'm glad God is more forgiving than I. What a murderer!" The afternoon sun was shining brightly, casting dark, accurate shadows onto the cobblestones, which deflected and broke up the lines into squiggles. "Shall I get a cab for you? I always have an easy time getting a cab," he said, adjusting the painting beneath his arm. Then he added, *sotto voce,* "Paying for one, however..."

Simone turned back; in the lower window she saw a face—a face like two brushstrokes in an Old Master painting, disappearing when looked at closely.

CHAPTER SEVEN

Nazis came to interrogate Emile. Emile opened to the knock at the door to find a lieutenant and a corporal—the same corporal, from the border control, who had said he would see him again.

They saluted cursorily, limply; there was no clicking of heels. The lieutenant looked baggy-eyed and worried; the lining of his jacket was falling out. The corporal had a cigarette twisted like a screw into the side of his mouth.

"*Gute Morgen,*" the officer said. "Please let us in?"

"What do you want?" asked Emile, in his doctor's smock.

"We are investigating the death of Major Heinrich Schrödinger. You are under suspicion of deliberate malpractice."

"Gentlemen, I am rather surprised. Please come in nonetheless. Whiskey?"

"Not so early," said the corporal.

"I'll have a glass, please," said the lieutenant.

"I have a patient in the back; I'm afraid I can't keep him waiting forever."

"This shouldn't take very long, if you have the right answers."

"How are you, Doctor?" asked the corporal, still chewing on the same cigarette. He clearly meant to smoke it all the way to his lips; there were blisters where he'd already done so.

"Business could be better," he said, giving the lieutenant some whiskey.

"How did you come across this whiskey?"

Emile smiled. "I took a patient off of alcohol in order to save his stomach. Out of gratitude he gave me what he couldn't have himself."

"What did he pay you with?" said the lieutenant, sniffing at the drink cautiously.

"You're about to have his payment," said Emile, still smiling—the rubber smile Simone hated. "Simone!" he called, stepping into the back of his office and opening the doors that led to the living room. The door was invisible on the other side. "Simone!"

"Is that *meat* I smell, Doctor?" asked the lieutenant.

"No—burnt vinegar. Simone is a very handy

cook, a great illusionist. Simone!" She appeared wearing a cook's smock. "Take René out for a walk."

"Emile, I'm cooking."

"I'm getting interrogated by two *officials,* and I won't have my son hear. Out," he said.

Simone undid her smock and dropped it on the floor. "Come, René!" she called.

"And you have a cook!" said the corporal.

"She's my secretary. We get by."

The lieutenant had sipped the whiskey. "Not bad. How much did you get for operating on Major Schrödinger?"

Emile sat down and pursed his lips. "May I see the documentation giving you the warrant to ask me these questions?"

"May you...?" the lieutenant smirked. "I don't have the documentation. There isn't any. This is an informal inquiry."

"We're just trying to scope things out," said the corporal. "Make sure everything's ship-shape." He waved big-knuckled fingers around; the cigarette wobbled in his mouth.

"Let me talk, would you," the lieutenant said. "Take notes." The corporal nodded quickly.

"Comes down to this," said the lieutenant, finishing the whiskey. "Either you give me what Schrödinger gave you," he said, "or I file a very unfavorable report. You might get arrested."

The corporal kept on staring ahead dispassionately. The cigarette kept burning; it would touch his lips soon.

"Well, Lieutenant..."

"You do realize, don't you," said the lieu-

145

tenant insolently, "we're both former Gestapo." But Emile smirked.

"Major Schrödinger had an ulcer the size of your fist. He promised me four hundred Deutschemarks. But I only got two hundred. The balance was to be paid upon his recovery. Shrewd. Who gets to keep his money now? You?"

The corporal and the lieutenant looked at each other. "Okay, Doc," said the lieutenant. "We'll give you a deal. Give us the two hundred..."

"...and some cigarettes..."

"Some cigarettes, some whiskey, yes, I understand," said Emile, waving out further demands with a brisk wave of his hand. He slouched in his chair. "Not getting paid?"

"Haven't received a paycheck in the past two months."

"I'm sure it will all work out," said Emile. "Shall I write you a check? To whom shall I make it out? Would you prefer separate payments?"

"Cash, please," said the corporal.

"I was always sure we'd meet again, Corporal."

"Sorry about this, Doc. I meant to come, really."

"What happened?" Emile said, reaching into a wallet and taking out the Deutschemarks. He extended them toward him.

"The end of the war happened. Naw, Doc. Hand it *all* over." The two men got up. The corporal had a truncheon. "C'mon, Doc, we don't want no trouble."

"My ration card's in there; I don't care to lose it."

"We won't need it. Not where we're going."

"Oh. Deserters."

The truncheon came down hard on the back of Emile's head.

In the street, René pulled and grasped at Simone's hand. "For God's sake, Simone! I don't want to be held by the hand anymore! Let go!"

Two Wehrmacht privates sucking on sweets walked by, watching with amusement as Simone fought a flailing, twisting René.

"My, my, son difficult you have."

Simone smiled bravely.

"Your son, is he?" asked the other.

"Yes, yes, he's my son. Only he's not very well behaved."

"I'm *not*!" yelled René.

"Child awful."

"In badly need of military training."

"Eh, you!" said a passerby. "Haven't you two anything better to do than pick on a poor French boy?" It was a Frenchman in a hat.

The two Germans looked shocked, and then looked at each other. "Pardon, pardon...." They lifted their hands, candies in each, to indicate blamelessness. "We haven't done anything wrong, have we?"

The sour-looking man, wrinkles all over his face, glared back beneath his hat. "Yes, well, you'll see. Just you two behave!"

The first private did a mock salute, turning

it into an obscene gesture when his fingers touched his visor.

"Kitchy-poo," they said to each other and to René. "Sorry; we are so dangerous, you know."

"*Ja,* look at our terrible weapons!" said the other, brandishing his lollipop. They grinned idiotically at each other and walked on.

"I'll stab you with my lunch!" cried the first.

"France will be on her knees when they see my *sucette.*" A good-looking girl walked by. "Ahh," they said, raising eyebrows and sticking their suckers deeper inside their mouths.

"How old are those boys?" someone asked. "Sixteen?"

Two years older than I, thought René, still hanging on to Simone's hand. He jerked it free.

"René!" she cried.

Just then a bourgeois family came by. They were walking along, in circumspect, Nazi-approved black, looking unhappy; the man, dour, the woman, sour, and the children sullen. They passed by, the couple in one motion inspecting her head to foot and then walking on. The adults didn't even look at the nearby pastry shop, full of goodies made with ersatz flour. The children tried, but were corrected by the mother, who placed a hand on each soft head and rotated it, like a driver turning a screw, so that the children faced forward, right down the walkway: march, march, march. With butter now at nine hundred francs per bar, it was doubtful even they could afford it, Simone thought.

René had broken free and began dashing down the street, after the German privates, who had gotten into another shouting match with some civilians. The Germans were getting pissy. Simone cried, "René?! *René??!!* RENE???!!!" desperation and reproach rising in her voice each time she repeated the name. Suddenly he was gone.

Simone, with a horrified hand over her mouth, dashed down the street, conscious of all the bourgeois looking at her from windows. And she moved from window to street to shop to anger to despair until finally she stopped, held her head high, and, ignoring the looks that men gave over their shoulders as they admired her face, her figure, her lips, her downturned face, collected herself. Appear, she demanded of him. Appear, wherever you are.

René was watching her from behind a pot in which a delightful lemon tree was growing. It had been stripped of all lemons, of course, but no one had as yet swiped the tree. It hid him easily, and in the crowd of blackly dressed bourgeois it was easy to hide. He saw Simone bury her head, running from shop to shop. That was enough punishment. And he needed her to get home.

Now she was walking coolly, elegantly, and even though René knew little he was beginning to become aware of the attention she drew; men looked away from the wives they held in their arms. When she saw him standing with impunity next to his hiding place she walked up to him and slapped him.

"That's for running away from me, making me look like such a fool in front of these people. You're lucky if I don't tell your father."

Emile, sprawled on the floor of his office, was having a nightmare:

Simone knocked at the door. "I've brought us some bananas," she said.

"Oh, isn't that lovely!" cried Emile with the children, who had tied his wife to the dining-room table. The inscription had been changed to read: "You, whoever you are, shut your mouth, listen, and eat with gratitude. For this is the body and the blood of Our Lord." Maman Marie was gagged, but no one paid attention. Florence, the maid, was in a white-and-blue apron with metal spikes, and when Simone took out the bananas they were all made of solid gold.

René unpeeled one and began eating it. "No!" Emile cried. "This way." And Emile put the ingot in his mouth, and began sucking at it, closing his eyes, sucking lovingly, tenderly, enjoying the inert taste of the gold, its cold perfection; its inedible cruelty....

"Don't you think we should melt some down and feed it to Maman Marie?" he said. His mother walked in from a nearby closet and nodded her head silently. Suddenly the room was full of priests, all of them rotating in place like gears in a car. A barrier came down on his head. "Halt!" he heard. "HALT!!"

150

• • •

He woke up. Simone was looking at him. He gave out a cry, and he reached for her, but his arms couldn't move; he did not feel awake; she did not seem alive; the entire room seemed insubstantial, no more real than his furious dream.

"Emile!" she cried, and dropped beside him. He was awake; his eyes were opening and closing slowly, like a fish's mouth.

"I am all right," he said. "I got the better of them. Really." Then, after a pause: "Get out. I must recover. Out! Out!"

In his office, Emile took out a sheet of paper—not the creamy stationery he was still hoarding, but the ersatz wrapping paper—and began writing:

My dear wife,

And then stared. What could he say? Stop throwing away cash on horse races? Why the hell won't you offer the kids lodging and food till the end of the war? Your wine's horrible, can't you sell it as vinegar? To Nazis, even? Marrying you was the biggest mistake of my life. He crumpled up the letter and threw it into the rubbish bin. He stared, numb, straight ahead at nothing. Then he retrieved the letter, smoothed it out on the desk, and with a medical razor that he kept in the desk cut out the date and salutation. These he burned with a match, dropping ashes with satisfaction into a bronze saucer. He put what was left of the paper, a little smaller than before, back in the stationery pile. And took another clean sheet.

Last Will and Testament

He scrawled across the creamy stationery from before the war, using a black-as-midnight ink, not watered down for once, like the milk or the coffee or the wine or the morphine.

Beneath the drawer of the desk was a false bottom: he lifted it and pulled out his most recent last will and testament. This one dated from before his marriage, and had in fact been also arranged by their matchmaker. The old fraud had notarized it himself, thought Emile, looking at the dead man's elegant, patrician signature, and comparing it sadly and humorously with the scrawny, nervous dribbling he'd scratched into the page. The nerd, thought Emile, intimidated to death by the quill of the upper class. Upper class, my ass, he thought with a smirk, and with a smile began rewriting the pompous opening of the will.

Then he heard Simone banging, banging on Paulette's door. He heard her voice, her shouts. His pen stopped in midair, in mid-sentence, in mid-word—he didn't dare touch the creamy paper with the harsh, trembling steel. Still the clamor continued. Write, Emile, pay no attention; but his hand refused to obey. His hand shaking, he put the pen back into its well like a sword into a scabbard, and got up. Outside there was still banging and wailing. He took the key from his waistcoat chain and opened the dispensation cabinet. Medicines and drugs and razors and scalpels lay in their perfect order; this Simone was good at. He took a syringe—a good, sharp one, nearly new, and a bottle of morphine. He took off his coat as he heard the wailing on the children's door. To treat the children so badly! He bared his sleeve. Bang bang bang. He wrapped a tourniquet around his arm, tight; he didn't want to miss the vein now; he wanted his brain calm right now. Emile, he commanded, don't listen to her. The needle went in. Yes, he thought, and closed his eyes. It sounded like the sea outside, like waves throwing themselves uselessly, endlessly, soft as rain.

"Emile?" Simone asked, rapping gently, feebly, on his door. "Emile?" Simone started twisting the doorknob, but it wouldn't turn. "Emile, please open the door," she said. "Emile? No matter what happened, Emile, you shouldn't lock your door on *me*. Emile, please. I'm all alone, too. You can't—mustn't—shut the door on me; I'm *trying* to help. I'm only the cleaning lady. I am the secretary, the cook, everybody except your wife—who treated you so badly." She screamed. "Open the god-damned door!" And with the heel of her hand she hit the door hard. Then she fell to her knees at the door and lowered her face as if in prayer and agony. "Emile," she continued, more quietly, between breaths. "Take pity on a poor mistress. Have compassion on a worthless whore, a loser in the game of ladies. I beg of you, in the name of all I have ever done for you. If ever I have shown kindness to you, Emile, please, please, please, open the door."

Still the door was shut. Simone stood up, wiped her eyes, and then began banging with her fists upon the door. "Goddamn you! Goddamn you!" she cried. Then, smiling: "Emile, it's me? Remember? Simone? Who lives here? Can I come inside? What are you doing in there? Hiding Jews? Counting money? Are those Germans still here?"

He spoke from behind the door. "Simone. Leave."

"Your children are here. Your children, Emile, whom I raise, whose clothes I wash, whose food I cook, they're out here, wondering what the hell it is you're doing in there."

"Leave me alone. No one can help me. Go."

René spoke. "Paulette says someone tried to violet her."

Simone asked: "Violet?"

Paulette nodded solemnly.

"Violet?" she asked again, and laughed. But Paulette was not smiling; it was not a joke.

Simone waited, fully dressed, in the bedroom, for Emile to emerge from his workroom. Both children were in bed. She had left both their doors open; she could hear and see them should they venture up. And the children could hear and see them.

Around one-thirty, Emile, still in jacket, tie, and vest, opened the door from the office, which he'd bolted shut.

"Simone. You're still up. Why?" He did not look her in the eyes.

"I don't like sleeping in a cold bed."

"Get a bed warmer."

"The war has made fuel so expensive—and wouldn't it be extravagant, burning fuel in summertime?"

"It's hot in here."

"The windows are open."

He loosened his tie. "Simone, have some pity on my nerves. I've been working until late; I don't want to have an argument. Why is the door open? The children might hear."

"So what? Besides, it creates a breeze, don't you think?"

"Close it."

"No."

Emile stood stunned. " 'No'?"

"Close it yourself."

"Simone, what's wrong with you?"

"Emile, what's wrong with *you*?"

"Work. War—have you noticed?"

"Your daughter has a different opinion. It turns out some man grabbed her thighs and her arms so hard they left bruises, and all you can—"

Emile had put his hands over his ears. "I have had enough," he said loudly, while she kept on talking.

"—do is not listen, tell her it's her fault, it's always our fault, it's never you who are at fault—"

Emile scrunched all sound out of his face, closed his eyes tightly as bomb blinds. He glanced at her to see if she was still speaking. She'd stopped, watching him, though, like an archer behind a slit. She was saving the best for last.

"Stop," he said quietly, lowering his hands to his sides, and slowly, as if under water, reaching up to unfasten the tie from his neck, which hung like a loose noose.

"And taking morphine," Simone said simply. "Slurring speech, general incompetence."

"Simone, I have a lot of work tomorrow—surgeries, patients—"

"Your first appointment is at two in the afternoon. You arranged to have the morning free to do work."

"Well, then maybe I'll need to see patients anyway!" he yelled. "Don't tempt me," he said, raising his hand to her face.

"Go on, Emile. Let's see the valedictorian lose to a poor unschooled prostitute."

"You are not a prostitute."

"Why do I get treated like one?"

He slapped her. There was a long silence while the house absorbed the cruel sound.

"There. That's how a wife gets treated. Do you feel better?" she asked. She stood up straight. "I bet you slap prostitutes too. You would. Go on, hit me again. What are you going to do next, cut out my tongue? Is that your answer for everything, force? You admire Germans so much; you treat so many Germans. We've all lost, but you—you lick the conqueror's boots. You slaver over Germans, you swear in German, you espouse their music, their philosophy, their politics. You curse France; you curse me!" She was crying. "Meanwhile, *I* stay here, I mind the house, and the children, I work for nothing. And no one."

Simone dreamed:

Suddenly she was in front of the brick wall, acutely aware of how much it resembled living tissue, with its pores, its strange openings, the roughened, wrinkled edges of stone, where time had worn away and left little messages. She was standing next to Sylvie, who was breathing deeply and quickly, in a panic. Several of the women had been crying and she had heard a Nazi yell "SHUT UP!!" so everyone was trying to be quiet.

"Ladies and gentlemen," she heard the lieutenant say to the crowd behind the cordon of storm troopers, "we are going to identify a member of the Resistance and deal with her appropriately. All right," continued the lieutenant, "which one of you females is Simone?

"No answer? Very well." He took out his Luger. "I will begin killing you ladies, one by one, until Mademoiselle Simone identifies herself. The sooner the better. If you are so unlucky as to be the first woman I kill, then the other six will necessarily die as well. If you give yourself up *now*, you will be arrested, but the other women will go free. It's up to you,

Mademoiselle Simone. We have your husband.

"All right," he continued, holding the Luger near his head, near his ear. "Safety is... off. I will count to three. On the count of three, I will kill you, on the left. I will leave the body right where it is and count to three again, until I have Simone. Clear? CLEAR? ONE!"

"Please, NO!" Sylvie cried, turning, and running toward the officer with the Luger. He didn't fire, and she ran right up to him and actually punched his sleeve before a sergeant grabbed her and pulled her back.

"My husband! My *children*! Don't touch them!" She was sobbing, mouth great and open as in Poussin's *Massacre of the Innocents*.

"Are you Simone?" asked the lieutenant scornfully.

"Yes," she said, crying, sobbing, trying to wipe her nose and not being allowed by the sergeant holding her. Simone, in her dream, did not dare look around.

"Arrest her, Major?"

"No, let's shoot her here." With a scream Sylvie was dragged to the wall. A sergeant slipped handcuffs over her wrists. She wailed and wailed, screamed and screamed. The sergeant finally bullied her against the wall.

Simone, looking straight at the brick, was only aware of Sylvie's wildly contorted face, the strange ways the skin was wrapping up, savagely.

"Hold still, you others," said a sergeant.

A Nazi hand pinned Sylvie's neck to the wall. Then the Luger pointed at the back of her head and fired.

At the loud blast two other of the women began crying. "SHUT UP!!" shouted the sergeant. Still the women went on crying.

"And then they ask why we rule the world," said the lieutenant, putting away his Luger, still cool after only one shot. "Tell them they're not leaving until they stop crying."

The sergeant translated, badly. Simone was suddenly aware of the lieutenant next to her, his face so close he could kiss her—kill her.

"Did you know Simone?" he asked.

"No," she croaked. The other women went on crying.

"You're lying, aren't you?"

Simone's throat was so dry she couldn't talk. She whispered, "I didn't... know Simone."

"Oh, you knew her under an assumed name. But you knew her."

"Y-yes," she stammered, and began crying, sobbing, talking to this man while facing a brick, unfeeling and yet organic, even wise, wall.

"I think"—turning to Simone—"we had better take you for interrogation."

She woke up panting. The room was dark, Emile was at her side, breathing a deep, vinous sleep.

"Emile," she said. "Wake up."

Emile opened his mouth and took a long wheezing breath.

"Emile," she said. She hit him again and again, furiously, waking him up with blows.

"What! What! What! Air raid?! What? The children!?!"

"Emile—I'm in a nightmare!"

"Are we being bombed? Is the house all right? What about the *gold*?"

"Emile! Gold?! Is that all you can ever think about?!" She hit him with her small fists.

He opened like a lightning bolt, suddenly awake, alert, dangerous. He seized her by the wrists and hissed at her in the darkness. "Goddamn it, you listen to me. Today I was *beaten up* by two Nazis. Two Gestapo pigs came to my door, and I called them deserters, and they mugged me. And you come home, and you think I'm shamming when I'm lying on the floor. Now you wake me up, finally one night when there aren't bombs, and you tell me you're having a bad dream??" They stayed clutched together for a moment in silence. Then he said, "Listen."

They cocked their ears, listening for the drones of planes, the rumble of tanks, the wailing warning of sirens. But oddly, terrifyingly, the house was quiet.

"The one night we can rest, and you wake me up with imaginary troubles. Fine woman you make." He let her go, turned resolutely away. "I still have a bruise where the truncheon hit. I accepted my fate; I didn't complain or cause any trouble. You do the same."

He fell quiet and pretended to fall asleep.

Simone tried; but the darkness closed in around, isolated her.

Simone dreamed:
She sat in a cell at the Conciergerie. She was awakened brusquely, and when she looked up, she was looking into the eyes of a female warden.

"Get up," she barked. The guard slapped a pair of handcuffs on Simone and led her out of the cell. Down the hall they went, past cells where every set of bars held a pair of imprisoned eyes—human beings panting, thirsty, shocked, stunned.

Endless cells. Endless corridors. The electric light bulbs had been stripped and hung naked above every few feet of stone floor; brown shadows flickered in corners, behind doors, crept around gates like phantom guards on patrols, swooping out of nowhere.

At the end of the trip they were in a room where the guard snapped on a switch. The guard tethered Simone by the handcuffs to a pole in the middle of the room and sat down behind the slightly raised desk which commanded the best view of her. The guard shuffled some folders and then pierced Simone with a gaze. "Are you with us or against us?"

"I'm innocent," Simone answered.

"*With* us, or *against* us," repeated the warden, raising her voice with an irritated, scratched command.

"Pétainiste..."

The woman stared at Simone, stared hard,

took in her hair, the way her eyes were swollen, the pasty-looking skin that came from having missed a meal and being kept up all night. Her gaze started at Simone's face, descended down the neck, down the breasts, down her figure, down her arms controlled at the wrists by iron.

"You're not married," said the warden.

Simone did not answer.

"I asked you a question. Are you going to make me ask everything *twice*?" The guard spoke with the cigarette protruding from her blistered lips.

Simone's own thoughts had become gray, incomprehensible....

"No," she said, and sank to the floor. Presently she was aware of footsteps and a second pair of footsteps: Major Schrödinger, wearing Emile's glasses.

"Goddamn, she's pretty. Hm. We haven't time for a full interrogation. But let us see what we can do. Have her stand up, Nola, would you." His mouth was again cold, cruel.

"Stand up, *citoyenne*," commanded the warden. Simone could not.

"Stand up, please, or I shall make you," said the major, tapping a folder into order. Nola leant down toward Simone and wrapped her arms around Simone's and hoisted her up. Their tits touched; Simone was aware of the breath, the lips, next to hers, the eyes looking into hers, and a smile on the warden's lips; Simone reached toward the pole for balance.

"What is your name?" asked the major. The voice was tired. His eyes didn't meet hers.

"Simone. Heinrich, don't you *recognize* me?"

"Family name, you idiot."

Simone burst out crying.

"Family name!" yelled the major. "Talk or I'll have your tongue cut out!"

"Givry."

"You live at number 16, rue de Maubeuge. You are a...?"

"Housekeeper. Some... secretarial work for a doctor."

"Oh, bullshit. What do you really do?"

"My—my husband—"

"Your *husband*? You're married? Doesn't say that here."

"My—my—lover. Don't you see, Heinrich?"

"Shut up!" he bellowed. "You call me that again and I'll turn you over to our friends downstairs; they'll teach you some manners! Now stop whimpering, or Nola here will correct you."

Nola had the concierge's face.

"Emile... gets... bribes."

"Bribes?"

"No! No! Not bribes! Don't write that down! Please! Listen to me! He gets paid with food!"

"Legally?"

"I never see the coupons. I only see the food. I cook the food."

"Yes, I understand that, miss. You're a cook, you're a mistress. I understand everything. How did you get this gold?"

"What?"

The captain slammed his fist on the table. " 'What?' Look, what! Goddamn it—I don't wish to ask you twice. Now look, goddamn you. I want you to give me the right answer because I want to go to bed to see my mistress. My wife. I am not the enemy, Simone; believe me, if a pretty girl is an enemy of the Reich I couldn't give a fuck. I'll let you go and kill two Jews, of which I've got too many already."

Simone listened to the voice. It sounded so clear, so promising, so much like the major she once undressed and dressed. But when she looked up there were only the grim teeth, the hard, cruel set of the mouth, the eyes glittering.

"What do I have to say?" she asked—she asked the walls, she asked the stone, she asked everyone except the major; she asked the shadows.

The shadows answered. The voice entered her ear like a serpent: "Tell me you know nothing."

"I know nothing," Simone repeated.

Shapes, shadows were sliding across the floor, floating up between her legs, entering her....

"I know nothing... about the gold."

The captain scribbled a few notes and admired them as if they were the delicate, embroidered lace on an oil painting. So amazingly real...

She woke up, heart beating double time.

Silence. Far away, a rumble of tanks like distant thunder.

The children, in their room, had heard the slap—followed by the more incredible sound of Simone telling Emile she could not be beaten. The children listened, looked at each other. This was how an adult defended herself. They were so tense, they half expected shots to ring out. And when there came only a long, mummified groan, they looked at each other. René clutched his new secret tighter.

René had found two magazines and kept them hidden in his bed. The first magazine was *Je Suis Partout*. The magazine excoriated an outrage organized by Anglo-Saxons, Jews, and Bolsheviks: someone had cocked and thrown a hand grenade in a Wehrmacht canteen. The Jewish community was to be fined a billion francs. All Jews should be arrested immediately. The second magazine René had never seen, nor had it ever appeared before: *France d'Abord*. It also described an attack on a Wehrmacht canteen, but it did not blame the Jews. It said the grenade had been thrown by a French hand, the hand of the future, the hand of the Resistance.

CHAPTER EIGHT

Paris began to fall. The Germans began leaving amid cautious, ironical smiles; generals with monocles sped down the Champs-Elysées; troops tried bargaining away a last pair of boots. Paris held its breath.

René's view of the Liberation happened downstairs, on the rue de Maubeuge. A Resistant came to have lunch with a rifle over his shoulder. He was a young man, tow hair peeled back like an onion, and the rifle was a Hotchkiss recuperated from the Nazi truck collision at Clichy. He wore a loose-fitting white shirt, and when he came stamping down the boulevard, men and women leaned out of first-story windows and waved their babies at him. To everyone he nodded seriously, keeping one hand on the sling; at his waist were seven cartridges. The rifle, people remarked, had certainly been fired. He didn't wave or raise his hand or salute: he wanted to look as much as possible like a civilian, and hand raising of any sort looked Hitlerian. Instead, he shook hands with everybody, left hand still clutching the sling, and the face serious as any face in Delacroix's *Liberty Leading the People.*

He sat down at a café downstairs from Emile's office; he was a local boy, and he wanted to show his mother he was all right. The owner of the best brasserie all but cleared out the restaurant to make sure he not only ate free, but at the very best table. He had some difficulty deciding what to do with the rifle—should he eat with it, or lay it alongside the table, or hang it on a chair opposite? His face highly serious, he tried as coolly as possible various combinations. Finally he opened the sling and wriggled the Hotchkiss behind his back, draped from his right shoulder to his left hip; with the sling in front of him, holding the napkin in place, he looked like a soldier come back for lunch.

The owner lost no time advising him what to eat, detailing the wonderful, incredible things that were on the menu that day: bread and cheese and meat. He tried describing a rabbit dish and said he'd been saving a few rabbits in cages for an important occasion; he could have one cooked immediately. The young man, whose name was Guillaume, spoke very simply: "Please—I only want a very simple, very French dish." At this there was thunderous applause from all the neighborhood, which had gathered round the restaurant and peered in to see this angel of deliverance eat rabbit.

It was almost like a religious ceremony, watching him eat; because he had come alone, he sat alone. At one point his mother came, and when she approached he said, "Maman!" And again there was applause and cheering when the two embraced and kissed each other's cheeks. The mother clung to her son as if he'd returned from Stalingrad—Was he all right? Had anyone gotten hurt? Where were those dirty Germans now?

Emboldened by this, Guillaume turned to

the crowd and yelled, *"Les Boches, on les aura!"* Great War saying—"the Fritzes, we'll get 'em!" At this, really riotous applause and hugging broke free as if from a cage; people repeated the saying like a magical invocation, crossed themselves. Even René, enviously looking at the rifle slung over the young man's back, repeated the phrase quietly; it did have an incantatory quality. The crowd broke into "La Marseillaise," and Guillaume, for the first time, broke into a smile—a real war hero. René bit his lip.

"Slut!"
"German-fucker!"
"Collabo! Collabo!"
"Cut her hair off!"
At almost the same time as Guillaume was returning to the front—avenue de Wagram—Josiane, the concierge's daughter, had been set upon by the same mob. The cries of delight, the smiles at the young man with the rifle and the cartridges turned to howls of sneers, disgust, and taunts. Josiane, who lived in the same building as Simone, had made no secret of her affair with a white-suited lieutenant. In his white gloves and white suit, pure as Lohengrin, he'd often paid her visits. Now that white was stained, nothing but stain.

"Cut her hair off!" they cried. When Josiane stepped into the street, walking quickly to avoid notice, first the women began following her, yelling "Whore, whore, whore," and then the men, smiling, fascinated by so easy a victim, so obvious a blemish to be wiped from the past, followed her, menacing, happy to finally play the cat in the game the Germans had been playing for the past four years. The butcher produced shears suitable for clipping wool, and a young man in the neighborhood, a sort of child's bully, waved the shears before her face, clipping as if they were the steel mouth of an obscene creature. Josiane tried to walk faster, to pay no attention, but the women, the boys, and finally the men following her surrounded her with sarcastic smiles and clouds of wolf whistles. Finally the women set upon her with nails and sharp hands and pulled her down to the ground. Eighteen years old, Paulette's age, but not Paulette's friend, she grimaced as women grabbed her hair and yelled, "What pretty hair for a German, eh?" And she was dragged over to the butcher's, who with a smile and remarks like "We're going to turn you into a good-looking *French* girl now!" and while she was held in place with the piercing gazes of the young women— some older, some younger than she—the butcher cut off all her long hair with a half-dozen snips. The haircutter, a sour, humorless man in a white smock, like a doctor at a concentration camp, arrived with an electric razor, a manual, and a strop. He was silent, but the crowd holding Josiane prisoner chanted, "Cut it off! Cut it off!" and as if he were attending a prisoner condemned to death, with Josiane sitting on the wooden slaughtering-

and-cutting block, held in place by countless small hands, shaved off every lock of her hair. When he was done, to general applause again, someone said, "Now Guillaume will find her attractive!" and kicking her and pushing her, they forced her back onto the streets, clutching strands of her black hair and yelling, "Collabo! Collabo!"

When Simone heard the commotion outside, she walked downstairs to look; Emile was in the office, doing something in the laboratory. She saw the crowd of people pressed hard outside the butcher's, and thought it was a queue for a meat ration that had just arrived; remembering that they had no meat—even the Bastiens had not eaten meat at all in the last months of the Occupation—she pushed outside. A young man, filled with spite and the exhilaration of power and denouncing, screamed at her, "What you lookin' at?" with so much force his spit flew in her face. Then she caught a glimpse of Josiane being shaved. Someone else, whom she'd never seen before, screamed, "Next we'll be doin' you!" She thought of yelling "Josiane!" but the deep wartime self-preservation instinct muffled the cry as sternly as if she were hiding in a closet while Nazis searched the house.

"Hey, isn't that Bastien's mistress?" another man shouted. Simone saw the eyes of Josiane, which permitted themselves for one second to escape from their sarcophagus of fear—from the mask of indifference and untouchability she'd encased them in—and she was desperate, asking for help, for intervention—for Simone to say *something*. But the mob surrounding her pressed too much; Simone felt arms, and muscles, and rough shirts split by years of overuse, all rubbing together like an animalistic mass, and with much more sense than idealism, tore herself away and made for the safety of her flat.

Three days later, at four o'clock in the afternoon, de Gaulle arrived, and even the tricolor flying over the Hôtel de Ville saluted. Emile went with his children to see the victory parade, like all Frenchmen who had had dealings with the Germans and who wished to be seen as supporters. If Emile could have demonstrated that he had listened attentively to the London broadcasts, had even punished his son for interrupting them, he would have; instead he wore a tricolor rosette in his buttonhole. He had considered wearing his old army doctor's uniform, but had grown too fat. René was too small.

De Gaulle came within only a few meters of them. He was tall, commanding—big stature, big legs, big nose—and the cheers and the waving, the feeling of elation, of welcoming the conqueror, were overwhelming—the ecstatic crowd kissed and hugged each other, strangers welcoming strangers, and anyone who looked dark, or Jewish, or infirm, was given a special smile, special words, congratulating them for having made it to what looked like the end.

Emile was arrested during dinner. First the telephone rang.

"Hello?" he said, sounding half cheerful, half cautious. "Who could it be?" he said to Simone and René.

"Doctor Bastien! It's me! Don't you recognize me?"

"I would like to," said Emile, charmed by the man's cheerfulness.

"You remember me? And my lovely girl?"

"No—can't you say a little more?" Then he added, aside: "Simone—an old patient of mine. I think he's calling to see how I'm doing."

"Oh, Doctor, I'm hurt you can't remember me. 'Frère Jacques, frère Jacques, dormez-vous, dormez-vous...'?" He began singing the childhood ditty.

"Ah, yes!" said Emile enthusiastically, still not quite sure who it was yet. "How are you? How goes the old problem?" A good question, a useful time-gaining tactic.

There was a knock at the door.

"Simone," he said to her, loud enough for his interlocutor to hear, "could you get that?"

René looked up from his bowl of lentils. Paulette was having dinner elsewhere—young, pretty girls had been much, much in demand the past few weeks.

The two young men who entered brusquely

asked to be taken to Emile. They were French—former soldiers both.

Simone smiled at them. "The doctor is taking a call from a former patient."

"That's what he thinks," said one of the men, producing a pair of handcuffs. He snuck up behind him. Emile was still trying to identify his caller, who still refused to say his name. Suddenly the line went dead. Emile looked at it strangely.

"Emile!" Simone said.

He turned around. "Ah, bonjour, messieurs. I have been the victim of a practical joke, as you can—"

"Emile Bastien, we arrest you on the charge of national indignity."

"What?"

"Of collaborating, giving succor, sympathizing with, and aiding Nazis during their occupation of Paris."

"Are you out of your mind?"

"No, sir, I'm doing my duty."

"What? Can I see your papers?"

"Certainly, sir." The older man, who had a Gaullist cross in his lapel, very solemnly pulled out a piece of paper. "Look here. That's your name, ain't it?"

"Yes."

"Well—then you'll have to come with me and my friend. Don't want to handcuff you, sir, but I will, so don't—"

"This is insane! What is the charge?! I'm not a collaborator! This is my son! I am a doctor!"

"That ain't for us to decide, sir, we're just following orders. Step outside, if you please."

"Who turned me in? Who?!"

"Come on now, sir, we don't want to get rough. There's a crowd downstairs that's plenty rough already."

And there was. The butcher's boy had seen the men arrive in what looked like an old army ambulance painted blue. The windows had been all blacked out. The crowd—mostly the same ones who had seen to Josiane's being shaved—were waiting at the base of the staircase. Some of the children had raced up the staircase and were waiting, with their shorts and sandals and hungry-looking bellies, to ambush the suspect on the way down. Among the crowd was Josiane herself, who now wore a beret to conceal her baldness; some disapproved, but others thought it a sign of repentance, and didn't mind because she was shouting louder than the others: *"Mort aux collabos! Mort aux collabos!"*—"Death to collaborators!"

The two gentlemen heard the crowd and saw the boys waiting like snipers along the staircase. "Oh, man, this is going to be a rough walk. I'm gonna have to handcuff you, Doctor; this is for your own good. The crowds don't like to see suspects with their hands free." And suiting the action to the word, he clipped the metal rings round the doctor's wrists.

"I have patients to see tomorrow!" Emile said.

"The judge will hear everything," said the man, forcing him to descend the stairs.

The boys started yelling, "Collabo! Collabo!"

174

• • •

Simone watched as Emile with surreal speed was transformed from a doctor to a traitor. Emile shot a glance at her of pure helplessness and fury. He was being led out the door. René watched wide-eyed as the impossible happened. Simone, too stunned to think, half walked, half staggered to the door alongside Emile. But all she could say was—

"Emile! Where is it?! Where?!"

He shot back a look of such venom and hatred she flinched as if from a blow.

"We can use it to buy you out!" she said.

The officer turned to her. "Listen, mam'selle. If I was you I wouldn't go about broadcasting that kinda remark. We all know the doctor's rich, and we know *where* he got his money. Don't do *no* good to go around yelling it on the rooftops. So I'd hush-hush if I was you."

"Collabo!" cried the young boy.

"Where is it?!" said Simone again, real panic kicking in, her face whitening, real fear draining blood down.

"Shut up!" said Emile, and turned to the staircase. "Don't listen to her!" he said. "She doesn't know what she's talking about!"

"Just walk straight ahead, Doctor, and don't pay no attention to the crowds. Just stare right ahead and pretend they aren't there."

The crowds were surging, boiling like a wave crashing down a mountain; and their voices were lifted in a collective screech of denunciation, their faces twisted in a grimace of hatred. Hands, fingers, teeth, all seemed to lunge at him, and he, hands behind his back, could not so much as lift a finger to shield himself from the barrage of insults.

One of the boys had crept into the flat and tiptoed straight to the dinner table, where he swiped both legs of the chicken and a handful of mashed potatoes. René cried "Hey!" and dashed after him; chased him halfway down the staircase, where the boy tried to melt into the back of the crowd following with joyful hatred the doctor on the way to the wagon. René caught the thief and tried to pummel him. When a chicken leg flew in the air, he yelled, "That's *my* chicken!" and then began a frenzied rush for the piece of meat, torn to shreds as hungry people deprived for months of meat tore strips from the leg and stuffed it into their mouths.

"Collabo!" yelled the other boy, and sloshed the mashed potatoes into René's face. René landed a blind blow into the boy's gut, and some adult wrested René back to position—wiping the mashed potatoes off his face and sticking them into his gob.

"Good potatoes, eh? That doctor eats well." The man released René, who was putting up a fierce struggle and was now at fourteen too big to be resisted easily. The man gave him a final shot, a kick in his ass.

"René, don't let them get you!" came the outraged scream of the doctor, before his head was forcibly lowered and inserted into the wagon. The crowd laughed.

Upstairs, another boy, having seen his

friend make off with a chicken, also tried to enter the flat; this time Simone, still pale with anger, intercepted him.

"Collabo!" yelled the little boy.

And Simone, with demonic fury, slapped the boy on the face so hard he fell to the ground.

"Get out! Get out! You animal!" Simone grabbed the boy's arm and hoisted, then dragged him to the door, literally throwing him outside on the staircase. "You urchin! Get out! René!" she called. "René! Come upstairs, *now*!"

She thought she heard laughter downstairs. For a mad moment she wondered—could it be real? Was it a practical joke—organized by that patient who had called earlier? Was it a joke?

And then René came running up the stairs with three of the neighborhood tough boys on his tail, his face caked with mashed potatoes and gravy, looking like he was wearing a primitive mask.

Simone could not sleep at all that night. Paulette had returned home late, around two, ready to make apologies. After four years of midnight curfew, the excitement of breaking it had not worn off. She was still a little giddy from champagne; to her surprise she found Simone and René sitting in the living room, every electric light in the house blazing ferociously, the house bright as a furnace.

"Simone? What's going on?"

Simone didn't answer. René looked at her

sadly. For once he knew something she didn't.

Paulette smiled, still feeling a trifle drunk, and broke into a giggle. "What?" said she. "Have you guys been all alone in here? All Paris is one big party, you know. You don't have to be young. Or even that old," she added, looking at her brother.

"Paulette," said Simone, "do you know if the police stations are open?"

"What?" Paulette thought the question hilarious and had to slap a hand over her mouth not to burst out laughing. "Police stations? Why?"

"I want to find out if I can I see him."

"See who?"

"Daddy," replied René.

"Daddy?"

"He's been arrested."

"Arrested?!" Paulette sank into a chair and then exploded into laughter, high-school-girlish and giddy. "You guys are certainly *very* strange. There are no more arrests. Paris is free. Haven't you heard? The war is over. Remember that man we saw down the Champs-Elysées? Charles de Gaulle? We're free, you know, we're French. Vive la France!"

"I should have known," said Simone.

"Should have known what? You people are not making *any* sense."

"Pucheu went to de Gaulle, de Gaulle had him shot. I should have known." She buried her face in her hands.

"Mother? What are you talking about?" Simone lowered her face still further.

"Daddy's going to be tried as a collaborationist."

"What?" asked Paulette.

René told her. "When you were partying, two men came. They carried him away. Papa will be tried. Possibly shot."

Paulette was quiet.

Simone started weeping. This time René immediately wrapped his arms around her, while Paulette looked on, stunned. René had been waiting for someone to hold, waiting since the war had begun.

At around three in the morning Simone could no longer contain herself and dressed. In the streets there were carousing, merrymaking, drunken students, drunken old ladies. Simone walked quickly; men whistled at her. She scowled at them. The nearest police station was about six blocks away, but it was a pleasant night in June and her wooden-heeled shoes were in good repair. Paulette would have an awful hangover tomorrow. Good.

So disorienting, this new-old Paris—no longer blacked out, noisy now, festive—but here and there she saw one of those damned posters beginning with AVIS. The Frenchmen now printing these notices of imminent military executions had not departed significantly from Nazi usage: the first word was AVIS, but the red-and-black color had been changed to red, blue, and white. It looked disgustingly like a menu—Under New Management. Things had certainly changed.

At the police station she walked up the stairs, transforming herself by force of will step by step.

"Mademoiselle!" said the police sergeant on duty when he saw her walk in. "It's a fine time to be alive, isn't it? What can I do for *you*?"

"Hel-lo," she said.

"Lost your purse? Your husband?"

"Oh, I don't know if you can help me." The sergeant was a jolly-looking man with clear blue eyes and a shiny bald head.

"Oh, no, no, I'm sure I can. Like some coffee?"

"Yes, please." She looked around the office. On his table, stacked, was a stack of death notices, freshly printed. She read the names upside-down: Emile Bastien's name was listed among others. At the top, like the catch of the day, was a well-known French police chief who had made things easy for the SS. Simone leaned against the partition for strength.

"My wife died in '42, you see," the sergeant began explaining as he fixed her coffee. "That's why I work the graveyard shift; I can't sleep at night anyway. Oh, it's tough, and I miss her. I wondered if I ever would be able to just—you know—love a woman again. Or even sleep again! Heh-heh-heh. But I look at you..." He was extending the coffee toward her.

"Oh, thank you *so* much," Simone said, and poured sugar into her smile instead of the coffee. "Tell me, what do you know about this?" She pointed to stack of posters, and then quickly drew back her hand so that he couldn't get a good look at it: her hands were much older than her face.

"Ohhh," the sergeant said, and his expression changed from hopeful boyishness to hopeless officer of the law. "Collaborators, poor devils. They thought the Nazis would be here forever, and they found themselves on the bridge when the bridge went up. Don't get mixed up in that, darlin'. Ugly business. Ugly business."

"Do you know where they're kept?"

"Oh, that's secret. Not a Nazi, are you? Trying to break someone out? Mata Hari?"

"Noo," said Simone, as Mata Hari–esque as she could be.

"Fort de Vincennes."

Too far to walk: a cab. And then? No matter; she went.

The Fort de Vincennes rose black, enormous, and was all stone, stone, stone. A beautiful, enormous tricolor flapped and turned about like a coquette in the night breeze.

Stone. Stone. Stone. And inside, Emile?

There were two guards at the door, bulldog-faced, leather boots gleaming. When Simone approached, one of them sounded a sound so much like *Ausweis!*" she drew back. She tried to recover the strength from the police station. "What do you want?" he asked.

"Good evening," she said. "I'm looking for a prisoner."

The two guards looked at each other. The sky was lightening: the washing of the sky had begun, with dawn trembling on the way.

One of them shook his head. "This is a fortress. No admittance."

"Please."

The guards looked at each other. "Name."

"Simone Givry."

"Are you a spouse?"

"No," she said.

"Daughter? Only family admitted."

"Please, you must let me in," she implored.

"No."

There was such quiet, and the fortress stood before her like a helmet with no eye slits: emotionless, unfeeling, pitiless.

"Please..." she said, and moved forward. The guards crossed their rifles to stop her. They pierced her with gazes strong enough to kill.

"Listen to me, you *pricks*," she said, keeping her hands at her sides, but wanting to rotate those barrels away from her breasts and use them to drown bullets in their hearts. "I want to see Emile Bastien, who is innocent, and a member of the Resistance, and a Chevalier besides, and I'm not going to be stopped by two adolescent flunkies who are afraid of a female. On midnight guard duty. Who do you think I am? Eva Braun?"

The corporal looked at the private. "All right—let her in."

The next barrier was final. Simone found herself at the desk of someone with a strange resemblance to General Karl Oberg, Höherer SS and Polizeiführer of Gross-Paris.

"The man you are looking for," he said, "is suspected of collaborating with the Nazis. He will be given a fair trial."

"How can a trial be fair if the outcome has been decided in advance?!" Simone asked. "I have seen—"

"If you insist on making life difficult for all of us, I shall simply ask you to leave. This is not a household, mademoiselle. This is the state, taking care of its citizenry. Some of us have duties. Good night."

"Look, you monster. *I* have *seen* a list announcing his execution."

"His name will be canceled from the list if he is found innocent." He added: "We find we save money that way. And since you've insulted me, I prefer you leave."

"I want to see the trial."

"No one may see the trial; they must be fair. Mademoiselle—the Nazis have treated us very, very badly, and these suspects have been accused of helping them. We will not treat them quite as badly, but we will certainly not treat them well. Now get out." And he turned to his paperwork.

A thousand words rose in Simone's throat: "clemency," "mercy," "charity," a list as long as the roll of honor. The man with the little glasses and the double chin remained hunched over his papers. She thought of bribing him.

"How much money would it take for me to see him?" she asked.

He looked up. "Quite a lot."

"Name it."

He leaned back and squinted at her, fingered with his thumb the cap of his pen. He didn't say anything, but he ran his eyes down her body like a zipper.

"Oh, is that it?" she asked.

He shrugged.

"Very well." She put her purse on the ground and, standing before the desk, looked him in the eyes. He sat there, piggish, powerful, safe, protected by the table and all its officialness. She put a finger on a button of her blouse, and her entire life with men flashed before her eyes. Was all this what it amounted to? Undressing for money?

She unbuttoned the first button. He had been leaning backward upon his creaky wooden chair; now he leaned forward and the old wood squeaked. Simone wondered and prayed: how much would he want? Her head was flushed with old images, half seen, half remembered, of strippers. She twisted her head sideways, hoping to show him the skin leading from her breast to her neck. How much would be enough?

She unbuttoned the second button and took a step toward the desk. "If you want to see more, show me Doctor Bastien."

He sat transfixed by that skin, swallowing hard, unable to move. "I can't," he gurgled.

"And why not?" she asked, wondering if there wasn't a woman who could get this man to obey, and looking around the room quickly to see if there wasn't a weapon lying around, even just the classical farcical rolling pin, to hit him over the head.

"Not yet," he added.

The thought of that immense fortress of stone, the labyrinth of stone, with Emile somewhere in it—inaccessible, unfindable—it was like a weight crushing her shoulders. She needed this man's cooperation. Yet there was so much pain in undressing for this creep: it was like pulling off her own skin.

He got up, waddled over and locked the door. Simone looked down at the floor. What am I doing, what am I contemplating? "No," she said to him, while the keys flew into the air, caught by fingers a couple of times. "First you take me to Emile. Then we... do it."

"How can I be sure you will? Or even that you'll want to?"

"I won't be able to leave the fortress, will I?"

The man thought about this. "All right," he said. "But," he added, "you can't leave now, can you?" And he took a step toward her.

"No—but I certainly won't make it pleasant for you."

"You don't have to make it pleasant, my dear." He grabbed a revolver from a shelf and slipped its sculptured handle into his palm. "I don't have to make it pleasant for you, either."

Simone looked at him harshly beneath black brows, her ebony hair like knives on either side of her face.

"Why don't you kill me, because I'm not going to do it with you before I see Emile Bastien."

He cocked the revolver.

"Go ahead," she said. "I'd like to see what you do with a dead woman in your office. Or would you prefer to have me that way?"

The revolver fired, making a deafening roar. Simone shrieked in fright; suddenly she was standing two paces back—she had flinched awfully. She was suddenly aware of her body, as in those moments of awesome pain or fear, as if it were dissolving: as if her limbs were falling down space, as if their physical presence were indeterminate.

"A blank," he said. "We use them to scare prisoners."

A doorknob creaked. "Commandant!" came a voice from outside. "We heard a shot!" But the door was locked; the gun was smoking.

"Yes," he answered. "I had a blank left over from the firing squad." He opened the door; in came the private from outside. He looked at Simone's open shirt. He also met her black gaze, and she turned away.

"Is she messing with you?" he asked. "Hey," he said to Simone, "don't fuck with him, understand? These aren't blanks in *here*, understand?" he said, waving the rifle barrel in her direction.

"Is he one of your executioners?" Simone asked of the commandant.

"What's she on about?" asked the younger man.

"She wants to see Emile Bastien."

"Who's that? The Gestapo doctor?"

Simone's eyes flicked upward, opening

wide and ears opening too, to drink every drop of this conversation.

"The one we're holding, yes. Could you take her to him? Give them five minutes together. Make sure she doesn't leave without passing through my office first. I'll have to—file a report. Listen to everything they say."

"Yes, sir," the private said, and saluted officiously. "C'mon, babe, we're gonna see your Nazi lover."

"Georges... I mean Private Blond. Treat the girl with some respect, would you?"

Inside the fortress, following the private, Simone imagined, or heard, wails and warnings going up and down the stone halls, resounding demands, blows, questions, in German, in French, the language of force.

The boy was talking ferociously. "You see, babe, you see, the reason, the real reason he has blanks, is 'cause the boys on the firing squad have to have their guilt alleviated. *Eh oui.* When the five of 'em aim at that red card on his chest, and shoot—blam, blam!—we're never sure who actually killed him."

He produced a large steel hoop, a key ring, and jangled the keys, then opened a metal door.

"Are you on the firing squad?" Simone asked.

"No—not experienced enough for that. Takes experience to kill a man, just like that, man after man, all afternoon long. Wait here."

Simone waited in the near-dark. Above her a single electric lamp glowed. Inside its transparent bubble the element seemed indescribably delicate; and Simone wondered why it was she had never paused to consider how delicate that wire, narrower than the pistil on any flower, wrapped inside a sheet of glass stretched as thin as paper, the whole suspended inside a vacuum: an airless house.

"C'mere," said the private, reappearing at the door. "I've woke him up; he's up and at 'em. Wants to see you. Follow me," he said, walking to the metal door.

Simone, in her haste, was wearing the foot slippers she normally wore at night only; and she was so quiet behind the youth's clunking footsteps that he had to keep turning round to make sure she was following him. Each time he turned round he twiddled with his rifle, cocked, opened, then closed the breech, or let the firing pin fall, or did something to the swivel, to remind her who had the weapon. And his Hotchkiss, Simone noticed, was the same model the civilian soldier Guillaume had carried.

"He's inside," the soldier said, pointing to a face-sized metal grille in the cold dark steel door. "Can't let him out. Talk to him here."

Simone approached the grille, covered by a mesh of wires, as in the partition between priest and lay in a confessional. "Emile?" she asked.

His face, swollen and puffy, was at the other side of the grille. "Simone!" he whispered; his voice was as dry as a dead leaf. "I'm hurt!" he hissed, speaking through dry lips.

She could say nothing. The soldier was watching and listening intently.

"Simone! Someone's been saying awful things about me—lies—Simone! Are you listening! Is that you?"

"Yes, Emile. It is I."

"Are they going to execute me?"

"Emile, I do not know."

"What day is it?"

"Emile," she said. "Where—is—it?"

"Where is what?" he asked.

"Our secret!" she said, and the young guard fingered his rifle again. "Emile—our dowry."

"Oh, God!" Emile wailed. "Oh, God, God, God! What have I done? Lies, lies, lies!"

"Emile! Where is it? I only have a minute more!"

"Simone—the prefect! He's helped me before!" His voice was high and squeaky, like a mouse's. "Promise him—whatever you like!"

"Emile—WHERE—IS—IT?"

Even through the grille Simone could see the doctor clutching his face in his hands with the utter desperation and misery of his position, possessed with speaking in riddles because of the nearby soldier. Simone knew then Emile had never trusted her—that this uncovering of the secret might unite them, like a proposal of marriage....

"Simone," he whispered. "In the cellar closet. Behind the mops."

"Time's up," said the guard.

Simone looked down the hallway, the rows of doors, the electric lamps hanging at intervals down the tunnels. She knew these tunnels led straight to the commandant's office. The guard rotated on his heels with a clatter of arms and began marching her down.

"Simone!" he heard behind her, Emile making one last attempt to scream through the hole in his door. "The prefect! Don't forget the prefect!"

"Keep walking," said the guard. "Time's up." And just to make sure, he stood off to one side and let her pass. Simone looked at him with angry black eyes, but as she passed by, his face of flint stared straight ahead.

Soon they were at the commandant's door. "Go inside," he said.

"Just a moment," she said. She still had her purse. She was almost shaking, but by haste and gritting and grinding her teeth she kept muscular control over her fingers. She pulled out a little mirror and a stick of lipstick. She painted her lips slowly, elaborately, knowing this feminine gesture would reassure the poor private, who stood with his machine gun at port arms, right hand inches away from the trigger.

The boy was transfixed. Behind his sealed lips his jaw dropped; Simone could see his face get longer. Now, she thought. She put away her makeup, cleared the distance between them with one step, and, closing her eyes, pressed her lips against his. The barrel of the cold rifle nestled between her breasts. She kept her hands behind her. Oh, to kill him, to have that weapon.

She stuck her tongue into his mouth and played it along his dirty teeth and swollen gums. She flicked her eyes open for an instant: his eyes were still open. But the vacancy had become dreamy; a primitive form of fondness and gratitude had crept into his face.

"We're not so dangerous, are we?" Simone said. The youth kept his hands on the rifle, and he was suddenly aware of how he'd used it, used it to separate himself from her.

"Must you still take me to your commandant?"

"I have my orders... mademoiselle," he added, respectfully.

"You know what he's going to do to me," she said.

"Yes." But Simone knew he did not. He was far too innocent to understand what a man could do to a woman with force.

Simone could see the dawn gliding across the door like a ship of doom. "Isn't it time for your stand-to?"

"Yes.... The firing squad will be here soon, to start work." Simone felt herself grow weak—she could faint, or pretend to.... But he might bring her to the office anyway; the commandant wouldn't care, would prefer her inactive, unresisting... no...

"How horrible," she said.

Dawn kept sliding up like a curtain.

"We must, mademoiselle. We must do what we're told. We are soldiers."

"I do what I'm told. And I'm only a woman."

The boy, for the first time, cracked into a smile. It was a boy's face, perhaps not even eighteen; but the smile was that of a fourteen-year-old. He had terrible teeth.

"Maybe you could come in and watch," said Simone.

"Watch what?"

"The... show. Yes. Please. Come in the office with me. Just stay for as long as you want to. Please. I like you; I need you."

"No. It's the commandant's business."

She could touch him: but she didn't dare touch his hand; it might have meant touching his rifle. He might flinch, he might panic.

She pulled out her pocket mirror and checked her makeup one more time. Then she looked at him.

"Would you permit me... ?" The back of her finger rose like a slow sailboat up, up to his lips. Slowly, carefully, as if she were defusing a bomb, she drew her finger across his lips. He was standing stiffly at attention, eyes flicking madly, unable to decide if he should stare straight ahead or watch.

"There," she said, and smiled. "No more lipstick." She turned around to face the commandant's door. "Time for me to do my duty. Would you knock on the door, please?"

The private knocked on the door with the butt of his rifle. It opened; there was the commandant, his sleeves rolled up. "About time," he said.

"I'm delivering the woman," said the private.

"Stand to. That will be all. Come in, you." He started closing the door. Simone gave one last look outside.

"Sir?" said the private. "Are you sure you don't need any help?"

192

The commandant gave him a look of total exasperation. "Go back to your duty," he said, and closed the door.

Simone looked around the room. There were no windows. They stood in silence. Outside, the dawn must be lighting the rooftops on fire.

With one brusque motion, Simone wiped her forearm across her lips and drained them of all their color. She strode to his desk and, with the same almost savage stroke, threw all its paperwork, pens, impedimenta down to the floor, sat down on the desk, lay on her back, hoisted her legs up, flicked her panties off, and drew her dress up.

"Do it!" she yelled, loud enough to be heard. "Do it *now*! Hurry up, Com-*man*dant!" She filled the word with a sergeant's sarcasm.

The commandant stood there, fully dressed. "You think—this is going—to intimidate—?"

"I don't want to hear excuses! That buck private took thirty seconds and we did it standing up. So drop your pants, fuck me, and let's get this over with!"

The commandant started unbuckling his belt, staring straight down her legs. Her voice had become screechy and insistent, like an old hag's giving commands to her husband.

"Get—a—*move* on!" she yelled. "Isn't it going to be stand-to soon? Isn't relief on the way? You must have firing squads and duties up the wazoo. I haven't got all day."

Half in anger, he pulled down his trousers and struggled with his complicated World

193

War I underwear. That open pair of legs kept staring at him. He waddled over, trousers around his ankles, grabbed her legs, and began bumping his crotch against hers.

"What is *that*?" she screeched. "You call *that* your manhood? I *demand* something of substance, this instant!"

"Look, you whore—"

"I am *not* a whore! I'll tell you what the matter is. *You're* not a man! A real man could do it *right now*. By God, if you were my husband I'd wonder who the hell you'd been with. Have you been drinking? But of course. What else is there to do on a long night shift? Summon that private, right now. We'll do it while you get *warmed up*. Call him, call him now!"

"You're mine."

"No, I'm not. I belong to all men. Now call him. It'll help to get some *young blood* in this room."

He pressed on a button that summoned help from the gatepost. A minute went by. The door opened. The private walked in, followed by a sergeant-major.

The sergeant-major, arriving to supervise the day's executions, looked around at the office, the mess on the floor, the woman on the desk, the commandant with his trousers round his ankles.

"Sir?" he said. "What the fuck are you doing? What the fuck is this? Who the fuck is this woman?" He walked over to Simone, put his hand on the back of her head, and with one clean motion scooped her up and put her on her feet. Instantly her skirt dropped down and covered her. The sergeant-major picked up her panties, which were lying on the floor, and smelled them. Then he gave them to her. "Get out of here, dearie." Then he dressed down the commandant: "You don't think, sir, your timing could be a little better? Thank you, Private, that will be all. Look at this shit!" Simone started walking away, but she heard him behind her: "No one minds if you fuck a girl in here, sir, but for God's sake, don't mess up the army's paperwork! We have a lot of people to liquidate this morning, and we need their paperwork! Now, sir, clean this up! Goddamn! What a mess!"

Simone walked behind the private. "Thank you," she said.

"I didn't do nothing." It was true: he hadn't.

"Thank you anyway." Both hands were still on his weapon.

"Do you think you could me get a cab?" Goddamn Emile for not teaching her how to drive.

The day's relief had arrived; sergeants were shaking hands and exchanging cigarettes. Everyone copped a glance at Simone and kept their distance: they assumed she was the commandant's whore for the night.

A cab—a real cab, not a pedal-pusher—came riding along; several of the soldiers began waving, jumping up and down; it turned in their direction. "Our lady getsh a takshi! Our lady getsh a takshi!" one of them said, in a harsh Auvergne accent.

The taxi pulled up and Simone walked

toward it. The soldiers, on duty now, kept their respectful distance. But the driver smiled.

"*Bonjour, ma chérie.* Where are we going?"

"La Varenne."

As soon as the door closed Simone felt safe. A real taxi—with a real motor. Inside Simone smiled. She had never felt stronger, had never so dominated a man. Where did she get this strength? Greed? She didn't love Emile anymore.

At the door of the house, still in the small hours of the morning, she went through her purse and found just enough to pay the driver; she threw out her ration card on the floor of the taxi.

In the house she went, and down the stairs. She knew what closet he'd been talking about. This last deed I will do for you, Emile.

As soon as she opened the closet she knew something was wrong. It was too small. And what a load of junk was inside! René had stashed some of his boyish things—comic books, toys— in this, the latest of his hiding places. There were two immensely heavy car batteries. There was a stack of coal, soiling everything; and the mops. There was nothing behind the mops— only the blank, pitiless wall. She began tearing through everything, quickly, yelling insults high in her voice, as if to insult the whole house; above her the electric light bulb burned feverishly and hopefully. Finally she realized. The car batteries. Of course. He had a thing for hiding the gold inside the car.

She ran up the stairs, barefoot—those slippery slippers were no good down here—and went to Emile's desk, to his phone directory. She dialed the prefect's number.

"Hel-lo?"

"Claude, wake up. This is Simone Givry, Emile's secretary." Somehow, the thrill of power that men wielded in a war—some of it was coming down to her now.

"What—time is it?"

"Claude, listen. Emile has been arrested. He needs your help. You must get through your channels. Is this line safe? The new government isn't still using the old wiretaps?"

"Arrested! Why?"

"Claude—we have an incentive. A substantial incentive. You must save him! He's going to be executed!"

"Executed!"

"Claude, call—someone, anyone—get them to stop the execution!"

"Incentive?"

"Gold."

And then, Claude said, slowly, sadly: "He is a collabo?"

"He is NOT a collabo! It's hearsay!"

"Simone—have you got something *besides* gold?"

"Besides—gold?"

"It's dangerous; tainted by the Nazis, some of it. Simone, you have no idea how things have changed. A collabo—it is too dangerous. You don't understand the delicacy of my position—"

"Delicacy?"

"They are looking for scapegoats—you've seen it. Emile was picked because he made too much money, treated too many Nazis."

"But they say he's Gestapo and he's not!"

"It is what a court of law can prove—Simone, this conversation is dangerous—"

He hung up.

Inside the batteries was acid.

CHAPTER NINE

Maître Bertrand Heidsick-Laval had been Emile's lawyer since he'd separated from his wife, and since then Heidsick-Laval had become the guardian of all Emile's secrets. The lawyer's office, high above the boulevard Saint-Germain, was in some respects similar to Emile's: there was a wood-paneled room where he received clients, a library where he did work, and one room where his secretary typed. Her name was Mademoiselle Gris. Simone noticed the girl, with a tremor of recognition and disgust, as soon as she arrived: a young girl, on her first job since the war, and no doubt, Simone thought with some scorn, providing extra services for Maître Heidsick-Laval. He had added the name Heidsick and the hyphen when the war had started—a move doubly fortuitous since the famous Laval had fallen. The poster announcing the execution of the most famous collabo after Pétain, had gone up some time after Emile's, and unlike Emile's had been timely. Emile's *avis*, saying he would be shot, had gone up two days after he was actually dead.

Simone had brought René and Paulette to the office. She still had not been able to sleep, except for a few hours during the middle of the day, and her eyes were puffy and red. Mademoiselle Gris looked at her as if at a sad old wreck. There were five chairs in the office before the desk of the maître: two to the right, in line, and three to the left, also in line. Simone had arrived first. She had placed René in the front row to the left, herself to the right in the front row, and Paulette behind her.

And then the door was crowded with darkness. It was Maman Marie, arriving from the south, dressed head to foot in an antiquated mourning dress from the south: a billow of black crinoline held together by a hoop at her ankles. Black hat with a veil studded with black tears cast a sort of haze over her face, as if she were visored and invulnerable. Dolores, too, was dressed in black—peasant black—her fat ankles wrapped in black stockings, black slippers, probably the same for puttering about the house, and a black dress. Simone wore lavender and gray—half-mourning—and it was a simple suit, not out of place in an office. She would play her role of secretary. Marie would play the role of grieving widow.

Marie moved over with a swish to Simone's seat. "Would you move," she announced, manipulating with dexterity her frilly black parasol.

"I stay here," said Simone, without looking up. She stared straight ahead.

"Impudent," said Dolores, in her patois accent. "She the widow, not you."

Mademoiselle Gris, looking like little more than a schoolgirl in an office, came over and stood behind the desk. She saw the tall woman in black standing, commanding, over the young secretary in pastel mourning. "Normally," she said, like a prissy schoolteacher, "the widow sits in front, and her retinue behind her, which is why Maître set the chairs up the way he did. Madame—" she said, looking at Simone.

"Mademoiselle," said Simone.

"Yes?" said the girl, not understanding she'd been corrected.

"I like this chair," said Simone.

"But it's not part of the *rules*," said the girl, irritatingly, screechingly, excruciatingly *comme il faut*: "It just *isn't done*."

"Very well," said Simone. "Where does the *secretary* normally sit?"

"At the *back*," said the little schoolgirl.

"So you see," said Marie, vowels low and thrilled with scorn.

Simone looked imperturbably at the lawyer's secretary. "And what about a close friend?" asked Simone.

The girl seemed confused. "Are you the secretary, or—the close friend, as you say?"

"I am both, my little girl," Simone said.

"Then she should sit—in the front row," said the girl. "Next to the widow."

Marie shot pure venom at the girl. "She is a secretary. Put her in the back."

Simone remained in her seat.

When Maître Heidsick-Laval arrived, Marie was sitting to Simone's left, with Dolores behind her. The children sat in a row behind their mother. René had quarreled with Paulette, briefly, for the middle seat, the one nearest his mother, but she'd held it fast.

Dolores refused to look at Paulette. Marie had bowed solemnly, full of form and empty of feeling. But she'd kissed René on the head and excitedly stated how much he'd grown.

The maître entered as stiffly as a judge. He was dressed entirely in black but for a blindingly white stiff collar. Over brand-new reading glasses—the war was good for the executor's business—he quickly stared at the assembled company as if they were his parishioners; a prim mustache hid his mouth. His hands, holding the will, were pale and crisscrossed with dark hairs. He sat down and coughed quietly, looked disapprovingly at the sunlight outside, and then flashed hard, silver-lined eyes at them.

"Ladies... and the young Monsieur Bastien. I shall be brief," he said. "First. Are there any questions about the provenance of the will?"

Silence.

"Notarized Paris, 1942. Would you contest the provenance...?"

Neither Simone nor Marie moved a finger. Dolores sat as still, as attentive, and as uncomprehending as she did at a Latin service. René fidgeted.

"Second. The will was drawn up while the invaders were in Paris, and was notarized with their accordance. Nonetheless the will is illuminated now by French law and French law alone. If you would have the will interpreted by other laws... ?" Again he let his voice draw out, and his eyes flicked over his glasses like periscopes over a windy sea.

"Third. Due to the circumstances of the death of Doctor Bastien for which you have, Madame Bastien, my deepest condolences—"

"Thank you," Marie said, and bowed her head in a perfect facsimile of grief.

"—the State takes an interest in the distribution of his effects. Any material which has not been declared in *strict* accordance with French law shall be seized, immediately, without contest. I am a servant of the State, ladies, and Monsieur Bastien, and am bound to turn over to France anything *hors de règle* I find in this will—and this regardless of Emile's intentions. Fourth, my commission is seven and a half percent, leveled on everything mentioned herein. Is all that clear? Are there any questions?"

Simone's face was tight as a mask. She nodded very, very slowly: it was a very false yes.

"Article one. Properties... Maubeuge and La

Varenne, and their contents, to the children."

"Maître," said Simone, "does that include the Chenard-Walker?"

"It says 'and their contents,' mademoiselle; the Chenard is contained in the garage, is it not?"

Simone did not nod: she looked at the ground acquiescently.

Bertrand continued reading. Marie raised an eyebrow and glanced from the very extremity of her peripheral vision to Simone, who'd visibly tensed even harder.

"Article two. Intangible holdings: stocks, deeds, bonds... to the children, held in trust governed by the maître."

"Does it say anything about precious metals?" Simone asked.

Marie's breath quickened; beneath her corset, seas were tossing, violently, powerfully.

"In a minute, mademoiselle. Article three: The medical practice. To be left to René. Young man—are you a doctor?"

René shook his head slowly, disbelievingly.

"Emile didn't say what to do if you weren't. Ah, well. We will proceed according to the Napoleonic Code—thank God we've got that back again."

"Nothing for me?" asked Paulette.

"Wait," said the lawyer. He took a deep breath. "Article four: Precious metals."

The silence, which until then had become extraordinary, became that of a tomb. Marie stopped breathing.

"Unusual clause," said the lawyer, becoming didactic. " 'To Paulette I leave the family silver.' "

A long pause. After a minute—Marie was as tense as a soldier about to go over the top of a trench—Bertrand looked up and studied them.

"*Silver?!*" Simone exploded.

Marie shot her a glance that would have caused a fresh sunflower to wilt, and took a series of sharp breaths. "My God," she said. Dolores crossed herself.

"That's all," said Bertrand, placing his glasses on the table.

"What do you mean, that's *all?*" said Simone.

"I mean that's all—there are no more provisions—no more articles."

"You haven't read the whole will!" cried Simone.

"No—you're right—I haven't," said Bertrand. The assembly fastened eyes upon him like jaws. "Emile was a clever man. He knew legal terminology, and so he wrote the will in a very lawyerly style, which is all but unintelligible to the lay. I said I would be brief. I've condensed it. You can peruse—"

No sooner had he said it—held the will up—than it was snatched out of his hand by an angry Simone. Marie sat in her chair, behind her veil, and her scowl seemed to spell the ruin of an empire. Slowly, while Simone frenziedly turned pages and checked each strangely spelled word, each unmistakably written in Emile's flowing, pulsating hand—

Marie lifted her veil from her face, as if she were raising the visor on a helmet.

"The old bastard," Marie said softly. Bertrand raised an eyebrow and then, standing next to Simone, looked down her breasts—then lifted his eyes at the young Paulette, of whose angelic face he had now an unimpaired view. Paulette looked down, embarrassed.

Marie turned to the children, rotating in her immense hooped dress. She smiled: very sincere-looking. "Well, children, Papa turned out very good and generous, no?"

"*N'est-ce-pas,*" said Paulette. Isn't that so.

René said, "I don't want to be a doctor."

"Well, young man," said the lawyer, "with this inheritance, you won't have to be."

"I an idea have," said Dolores.

Simone stopped studying the will—everyone looked at the old servingwoman.

" '*Argent*'—it means money. Family *argent.*"

"Yes, madame, '*argent*' does mean money," said Bertrand, primly. But the word here is '*argenterie.*' Silver. And it belongs to Mademoiselle Bastien."

"I assume you don't know where it is, either," said Marie to Simone. They were taking the taxi from the lawyer's, each with a copy of the will. René and Paulette had theirs in their hands. Marie had put her copy in an ancient-looking folder, no doubt one that had carried many similar wills. Simone had already folded hers and put it in her purse. She did not answer Marie's question.

"What's your guess, Simone? Maubeuge or La Varenne?" Marie was sarcastic with power. The children watched as the adults conversed. Simone refused to answer.

"Simone," said Marie, very quietly, and tactfully, and patiently, like a priest explaining original sin to a child, "you don't know where it is. You can't fool me, Simone. He hid it from you, he hid it from me. But someone must know." She looked at the children. René she stared back at with indulgence. Paulette she looked at severely. "*Someone* must know," she repeated. Then she turned to Simone. "Have you been looking for it? Hm?"

Simone still refused to answer.

"Well, answer me this, silly girl. Where are your shoes? Your clothes? Where have you been living? Because I'm going to have to ask you to empty all your things, immediately, from my late husband's house. Where are your shoes?"

"La Varenne," Simone whispered.

"Ah! You see, you're cooperative. Driver! Don't take us to the rue de Maubeuge. Take us to La Varenne."

"I think we should have some tea," said Marie, entering the parlor, looking at all the furniture. "Such a wonderful dowry. I'm glad I kept the best for myself, though. Dolores—tea, for four."

"I'm not sure there is tea," Simone said.

"Oh, make some from the sage in the garden, Dolores. Unless that Gypsy of yours, Simone, has stolen it all already. Naughty servants! Emile didn't know how to get loyalty. You don't either, I can see, mademoiselle." She looked outside the window, clutching lace curtains with her initials upon them. She grasped them with her thickened, wizened hand. "Hmph!" she said, and sat down regally.

She stared at Paulette. Marie began humming, softly, a childhood ditty—the same one Paulette had once sung to René. Then she spoke, reversing the words: "You know something I don't know. You know something I don't know. Where is it, Paulette?"

Paulette stared back. "You're not going to intimidate me, Mother."

"Oh, I don't know about that, Daughter. Do you remember how Dolores used to whip you? With a switch?"

"You can't do this to me, Mother." She crossed her legs.

Marie sat with her legs slightly turned to one side. "I want that money, Paulette. If you know, you'd better tell me."

René sat uncomfortably. Simone wore a strange, tense mask on her face.

"Simone!" cried Paulette. "Tell her she can't. Tell her it's wrong! She can't touch me. *You* can't touch me!" she cried.

Simone kept her mask at full power. Marie glanced at Dolores, who was still in her black clothes, standing still.

"Simone! Help me!"

Simone said nothing. She closed her eyes— as if she were closing a door in Paulette's face.

Her mother's gaze turned to Simone, with her closed eyes, and then back to Paulette, and then to Dolores, then back to Paulette, like a searchlight patrolling no-man's-land.

"I'm going to have you whipped if you don't tell me, because quite obviously *you know.* You want it all for yourself, along with the silver, the furniture, everything. I won't have it! You understand? This all belongs to me!"

"No it doesn't!" Paulette cried, close to tears while her mother kept a steady, powerful ogre's face, pitiless as an Oriental despot. "Papa said it doesn't! He said it was ours! His children's!"

René sat very still.

Marie observed blandly, "It was mine originally, I don't care what the law says." She sighed. "I will observe some of the formalities. The law is such an efficient mechanism for hurting other people, if you know how to use it."

Simone opened her eyes at this remark.

Marie continued. "But believe me, I will know where it is, and if you know where it is, you will tell me. Dolores."

The servingwoman, still unreadable as the night, took a half-step toward her. "Go lock all the doors in the house." Marie put Paulette beneath a spotlight of interrogatory intensity. "You of all people. Who helped him. *Daring* not to tell me. Are you saving it up for your boyfriend? I won't have you defy me, Paulette."

Dolores had returned, a smile like a skull's

on her face, a switch, good for making horses gallop, in her hand. "If she can make a nag walk, she'll make a hag talk. Tee-hee!" Marie laughed.

Paulette got up. "Don't you dare—"

With the speed of a mongoose, of a snake striking, Dolores held Paulette's small debutante arms in her big brown peasant hands, and a smile of vengeance suddenly graced Dolores's eyes and cheeks. The switch slashed—Paulette's head, her eyes watery, twisted round from the stinging blow. Simone looked away but did not close her eyes. René sat petrified. The house folded its arms in contemptuous quiet. Marie held her dark parasol like a Roman fasces.

"How dare you—!"

Slash! went the switch.

"Enough dilly-dallying! Where is it, Daughter?"

"Simone! Please! René!"

Marie looked at both of them. "No one will help you, Paulette."

"Wait! Don't—hurt her! Because—I know where it is," said René.

The switch hovered in the air.

He got to his feet. He was dressed in his best clothes—a dark suit, ill-fitting, like an insect's last chrysalis before growing wings.

Dolores glanced at him, panicked almost, then at Marie. "Let her go."

"Beat him, too?" asked Dolores in patois.

"No." Marie smiled, full of sugar and walnuts and honey, then turned that smile upon René. "Sweet son? You know where it is?"

"I know where. I don't know what it is," said

René. "But I know where it is." He looked around the room, as if his father would emerge to give advice. But nothing happened. The decision, the action, was his alone.

He led them down to the cellar. "I heard Papa one night—late, late at night—I couldn't sleep; I hadn't eaten dinner, again—he came down. Over and over, down the cellar steps. At first I thought it was a burglar. I was scared. But then I recognized him. He was carrying mortar. And bricks."

"What an unimaginative husband I had—have," she corrected herself, clasping the crucifix hanging round her neck.

He had taken them to the small closet and began emptying out the same cellar. Simone watched wide-eyed.

"You could smell it for a couple of days." Paulette shielded her face, checking for blood, watching as René emptied out the mess in the closet. "And then the smell was gone. Someone's been here."

"*Who's* been here?" asked Marie, scared and indignant, rising like a threatened lizard deploying its blood-filled collar.

"Here," said René. "This is where the new mortar starts." He pointed to the white, swirly mortar, looking as fresh as cream on a pastry. A square had been cut out of the wall, then replaced. "I always wondered what Papa had hid behind there. I used to hide things here too, so that when he went to check on whatever he was hiding he would notice that I was hiding things here, too. We would be hiding things together."

"Yes, yes. Dolores—get the pickax. We're bringing our baby back home."

While Dolores toiled downstairs, alone—you could hear the house shudder, clang, as if with rhythmic pains of giving birth—Marie went upstairs, gliding ghostly in her black robe, and dusted herself.

"Children," she said, "go pack. We are returning to Argelliers." Simone sat down. "You should go pack, too, Simone. And be quick; I'm not leaving this house before you do." She cast a cold, contemplative eye over everything around her, the vases, the urns, the mirrors. Then she looked at herself in the nearest, biggest mirror, admiring herself in the silver-and-gold frame. "An eye for an eye," she said. She looked appraisingly at Simone. "It was *you* in that closet, wasn't it?"

Simone lowered her head.

Marie continued. "Someday you will learn how to be a woman. You've a long way to go. Men and crowds are your enemies—or your accomplices. Think, Simone, of what might have been, if no one had denounced Emile."

The two women sat facing each other. There was a long silence, punctuated by the ferocious destruction of a wall downstairs, as if a film of stone was being pierced—a bubble of innocence.

"While you took care of that pig, I did what was just. God knows it was not a sin. I was indi-

211

rect—wholly indirect. It has made my world better, and France better, and that is all I have ever prayed for. What you pray for, I don't know. You poor hussy. He used you."

Dolores came up the stairs, heavy and slow. She'd placed the treasure in a box and carried it all up at once.

"Twenty?" asked Marie.

"Twenty!" replied her servant cheerfully.

Marie stood up. "Dolores, I want you to board up every window, make this house impenetrable. We don't want any thieves." She looked at Simone. "I will tell you one more thing, Simone—why I am not afraid of your knowing what I have done. I know about you and that major. The eyes of God have seen far."

"Father Nicolas... ?" Simone gasped.

"If the *least* thing happens to this house, or to my children, or to my property in Argelliers, I will see to it, Simone: you will be shaven, you will be humiliated, you will be run out of France for fucking an SS major like a seventeen-year-old whore. The *least* thing, Simone. You'd better consider it an act of grace that I let you leave with some dignity. I am showing some generosity. But remember—I have a sword over your head."

Something happened to Simone's face. She stood up, fixed her eyes upon Marie's. "Beware, madame—*la belle France* seeks gold. Maître Bertrand is looking for that gold. Seven-and-a-half-percent commission. One ingot and a half—not bad wages for one telephone call to the Ministry of War. You can hide it well. But the Ministry of War, to recover that gold hidden by the wife of a convicted collaborator, will rip up every centimeter of your precious property. They will punch holes in every wall of your ancestral house. When they're through, you will have to spend it all to give life to your murdered vineyards and your pierced house. Your little switch and your little witch don't intimidate me; your husband beat me a lot, and I have no fear of a little leather. So my offer is this, madame, for I also am inclined to generosity: five ingots for you. Fifteen for me."

On the day of Liberation, two searchlights that for months had scanned the skies for American and English bombers had been reunited, and back to back, kissing, they shot a giant V into the heaven above Paris: Victory. Now Simone, on the day of her own liberation, contemplated her still-pretty hands and with playful fingers shaped V, lying down on a strange bed. The flowers smelled of victory. The Germans were gone: he was gone. Beneath the bed, fifteen golden monsters to regenerate her life. It was the beginning of evening. Outside the window, she saw the bright world at peace.

A000010b3b408b